The Chronicles of the Shattered Crown

Invisble Guy

Published by Invisble Guy, 2024.

This is a work of fiction. Similarities to real people, places, or events are entirely coincidental.

THE CHRONICLES OF THE SHATTERED CROWN

First edition. November 20, 2024.

Copyright © 2024 Invisble Guy.

ISBN: 979-8223129912

Written by Invisble Guy.

The Embers of Dominion
The Rise of the Hybrid King

The ancient kingdom of the Underrealm lay deep beneath the surface of the earth, shrouded in shadows and secrecy. In the vast, labyrinthine caverns, where the light of the sun never touched, the people spoke in whispers of an old prophecy—one passed down through generations, carried on the winds of time like an ancient curse.

At the heart of the Underrealm, in the darkest recesses of its subterranean cities, a seer named Azra of the Abyss sat alone in her chamber, her eyes veiled by the darkness that had long since consumed her vision. She was a blind oracle, but her connection to the ancient forces of magic ran deeper than most could fathom. Her sight was not through her eyes but through the pulse of the earth, the vibrations of the air, and the whispers of the forgotten gods.

In a trance, Azra felt a chill sweep over the stones of the Underrealm, a tremor that spoke of things not yet born. The ground beneath her quaked, and the air grew thick with the scent of something ancient, something terrifying. The earth had revealed its secrets to her—secrets she was meant to keep hidden, but which now demanded to be spoken.

In the dim flicker of candlelight, Azra muttered the words of the prophecy she had kept locked away for decades

"From the ashes of the fallen, a king shall rise. Neither man nor beast, but a fusion of both, he will walk the path of power. The kingdoms will tremble before him, for his reign will bring either salvation or ruin. The Hybrid King is destined to unite the fractured world... or to shatter it beyond repair."

These words were ancient, older than the Underrealm itself. The prophecy spoke of a figure who would hold dominion over all the realms, a being forged from both human and animal blood—a hybrid king. His arrival was not a matter of if but when, and the time was fast approaching. As the power of Ravenor, an ancient dark god of destruction, slowly began to stir beneath the earth, the prophecy became more than just a warning. It became a blueprint for the future, one that would lead the world into either an age of unity or an age of chaos.

The prophecy spread like wildfire across the five major kingdoms, each interpreting it differently, yet each feeling the weight of its impending truth.

In Solara, the kingdom of the sun, with its golden spires and fertile plains, the nobles were divided. Some believed that the hybrid king would be their salvation, a force strong enough to unite the fractured kingdoms into one powerful empire. Others feared that such a king would mean the end of their way of life, that his rise would signify the downfall of the established order. King Alaric, ruler of Solara, feared the prophecy more than he would admit. As rumors spread of strange creatures—beasts that moved like men and men who acted like beasts—whispers began to circulate about Aldrin, the young noble and skilled warrior, who might one day fulfill the prophecy.

In the Glacial Dominion, a harsh land of snowcapped mountains and icy fjords, the prophecy was met with a mixture of curiosity and fear. The Empress Kaela, a woman of icecold resolve, saw the hybrid king as a threat to her unyielding rule. She had worked too hard to maintain her dominion over the frozen wastelands to allow some halfbeast to tear it apart. But even she couldn't ignore the strange occurrences happening within her own borders—disappearances in the snow, rumors of monstrous creatures stalking the tundra, and the growing sense that something ancient was awakening.

In the Sandborn Lands, where endless deserts stretched beneath a blistering sun, the prophecy stirred up ambitions of a different kind.

Here, the people were survivors, hardened by the harsh environment. The nomadic tribes saw the hybrid king as a potential leader who could unite the fractured desert tribes into a powerful force capable of challenging the more established kingdoms. But the desert kings were wary—such a figure could easily bring both destruction and salvation in equal measure.

In the Silent Marsh, the mistcovered realm where secrecy and whispers reigned, the people felt the pull of the prophecy more deeply than most. They believed the hybrid king was a being who would bridge the gap between the hidden, mystical world of the underworld and the realms above. Vera Nori, the matriarch of the Marsh, had heard the prophecies in her youth, but now, as whispers of strange sightings and creatures appeared in the mist, she began to fear that the time of the hybrid king had arrived.

Finally, in the Underrealm, where the prophecy had originated, the shadows deepened. Azra had long since seen the signs—strange mutations in the creatures of the earth, unnatural shifts in the energy of the realm. The hybrid king was not just a prophecy; he was a necessity. And as Ravenor's influence grew in the deepest corners of the earth, she knew that the hybrid king would not come willingly. He would have to be forged, and his rise would be the spark that would ignite the world into a war it had never seen before.

The sun had just begun to set over the vast plains of Solara, casting a golden hue over the capital's towering spires and bustling streets. The kingdom was at peace—for now. Farmers tended to their fields, merchants haggled in the crowded marketplaces, and nobles gathered in their opulent homes to discuss the mundane affairs of the day. But there was an undercurrent of tension, an unease that simmered beneath the surface, unnoticed by most of the citizens. It was the talk of the courts, the soldiers, and the scholars—the prophecy.

Inside the grand hall of the Solara Palace, King Alaric sat alone, deep in thought. The massive oak doors of his private chambers creaked open, and his son, Aldrin, entered quietly, his footsteps muffled on the lush carpet. Aldrin, though young, had become a trusted advisor and warrior to his father, displaying both courage and wisdom beyond his years. His reputation as a skilled diplomat and swordsman had earned him respect across the kingdom.

"Aldrin," King Alaric said without turning to face him, his voice laced with weariness, "the time has come."

Aldrin's brow furrowed as he stepped closer to the throne. "Father, what is troubling you?" he asked, his voice laced with concern. He had never seen his father—once so unyielding and proud—look so defeated. King Alaric was a man whose every move carried authority, yet now he seemed burdened, almost as if weighed down by something invisible.

"The prophecy..." King Alaric began, his voice faltering for the first time in years. "I never believed in it—the hybrid king—not truly. But now... now it feels like we are running out of time."

The king turned to face his son, his eyes filled with a mix of anxiety and something darker—fear. The prophecy had haunted Alaric for years, ever since the seers first whispered of a king who would rise, neither fully man nor beast, a king with the power to unite or destroy all of mankind.

Aldrin's jaw tightened. He had heard the rumors, the legends that circulated the courts, but never had he imagined that his father—one of the most powerful men in the known world—would believe in them. "You believe it's real then?" Aldrin asked quietly, his voice steady, though his heart raced.

King Alaric sighed, rubbing his temples as though trying to erase the weight of his thoughts. "I don't know what to believe anymore. Strange things have been happening, Aldrin. Creatures unlike any we've seen before have been spotted at the edges of the kingdom. Beasts that walk on two legs, with eyes that burn like fire. The reports speak of people going missing in the forests—whole villages vanishing without a trace. And then... the hybrid king. His rise has been foretold in every kingdom. A king who will bring an end to the old order. A king who will be a fusion of man and beast."

Aldrin's mind raced. He had heard rumors, but to hear them spoken aloud by his father, with such conviction, shook him to the core. The hybrid king was no mere legend, no tale spun by drunken storytellers. It was real. And Aldrin couldn't shake the feeling that the prophecy was somehow tied to him.

"Father," Aldrin began cautiously, "if this is true... if the hybrid king is real, then we must prepare. We cannot sit idly by and wait for fate to determine our future. We must act—before he does."

The king's eyes narrowed, a trace of approval flickering in them. "You are right, Aldrin. The world is changing. But who will rise to claim the power? Who will be the hybrid king? That is what we do not know."

As the days passed, the tension in the capital of Solara grew. Aldrin had been tasked with a crucial mission to travel north, to the Glacial Dominion, and negotiate an alliance with Empress Kaela, the ruler of the frozen kingdom. The Glacial Dominion was a powerful land of ice and snow, where the harsh winters forged resilient people. Solara had long been at odds with the Dominion over trade routes and territorial disputes, but recent reports suggested that the Dominion was moving forces toward the southern borders—an unusual action for a kingdom known for its isolationism.

Aldrin knew that the tension between the two kingdoms was high. An alliance could mean the difference between war and peace for Solara. But the prophecy lingered over everything—its shadow falling on every diplomatic gesture, every political maneuver.

Before he left, Aldrin met with his mentor, Varun, an older strategist who had once been a general in the Solaran army. Varun was known for his sharp intellect and battlehardened experience, but more importantly, he had learned to see the world differently. A past injury had left him physically disabled, yet he had become one of the most respected minds in the kingdom. His wisdom was unmatched, and it was Varun who had helped shape Aldrin's sense of leadership.

"Aldrin," Varun said as they sat in the palace's war room, "this prophecy is no mere tale. It is the thread that ties the fates of all the kingdoms together. You must tread carefully. There are forces at play that you cannot see. Not all of them are aligned with your best interests."

Aldrin listened intently, his brow furrowed in thought. "But how can we be sure? How can we know which side to choose? If this hybrid king is truly out there..."

Varun interrupted him gently, his gaze unwavering. "The hybrid king may be a weapon, Aldrin, but he will also be a mirror. He will reflect the truth of the world—its greed, its desires, its darkness. What you choose to become, what you choose to believe in, will determine whether the prophecy brings salvation or destruction."

As Aldrin prepared to leave for the Glacial Dominion, the tension within Solara's walls reached a boiling point. Rumors of attacks on villages near the desert—creatures that could not be explained—fueled the belief that the prophecy was not just a warning, but a call to action. Something was coming, and Solara, along with the other kingdoms, was about to be caught in the storm.

Aldrin mounted his horse at the palace gates, his mind racing with questions. What did the hybrid king mean for the future of Solara? Was the prophecy truly a harbinger of doom, or could it be the key to a new world order?

The journey to the Glacial Dominion would be fraught with peril, and Aldrin knew that the fate of his kingdom, and perhaps the entire world, rested on the decisions he would make.

As the gates of the palace closed behind him, Aldrin steeled himself for the uncertain path ahead. His journey had just begun. The prophecy had been unveiled, and the pieces of the puzzle were now in motion.

The hybrid king was coming.

And with him, the fate of all would be decided.

First Encounter with Isla

The journey north was grueling. The further Aldrin traveled from the warmth of Solara, the more he felt the harshness of the Glacial Dominion settling around him. The cold wind cut through his armor like a thousand knives, the icy air stinging his lungs with every breath. As he crossed the border into the dominion, the landscape shifted dramatically towering glaciers loomed overhead, their frozen spires glistening in the weak light of the sun. The land was a vast, unrelenting expanse of white, punctuated only by jagged mountains and deep fjords that seemed to stretch endlessly toward the horizon.

The Glacial Dominion was a place of stark beauty, but there was a coldness that went beyond the weather—one that seemed to seep into the very bones of its people. The kingdom's strength had been built on the harsh winters and even harsher rulers. Here, survival was earned, not given.

As Aldrin rode through the narrow mountain pass that led to the capital, he couldn't help but feel the weight of the task before him. The kingdoms had been on the brink of conflict for years, and now, with rumors of strange creatures and a rising threat from the underworld, he was tasked with securing an alliance—an alliance that could either save Solara or lead it to ruin.

It wasn't long before Aldrin was summoned to the palace. Empress Kaela, the ruler of the Glacial Dominion, was known for her unyielding leadership. She had built her empire with an iron will, crushing any opposition with ruthless precision. But it was her emissary, Isla, who Aldrin would need to convince. Isla was a woman of great intellect and poise, a master of diplomacy who had been tasked with navigating the shifting allegiances between the kingdoms.

Upon his arrival at the palace, Aldrin was led to a large hall where the air seemed to pulse with cold energy. The walls were adorned with tapestries of silver and white, depicting scenes of warriors battling in the snow, and towering glaciers that dwarfed everything beneath them. In the center of the hall stood Isla, her dark hair braided and draped over her shoulder, her sharp features illuminated by the flickering light of torches. She was a woman of striking presence—her eyes were dark, calculating, and sharp, and she carried herself with a grace that belied the fierce intelligence she possessed.

"Lord Aldrin of Solara," she greeted him with a nod, her voice steady and controlled, as if weighing every word before it left her lips. "It is an honor to meet you. Your father's message was clear. We understand the importance of this alliance."

Aldrin studied her carefully, aware of the tension that hung in the air. The room was cold, but it wasn't just the temperature that made him uneasy—it was Isla herself. He could tell she was cautious, calculating, and didn't trust easily. Still, she had agreed to meet with him, and that was a step in the right direction.

"I'm glad to finally meet you, Lady Isla," Aldrin said, his tone respectful but firm. "I believe that together we can secure a lasting peace. The prophecy is stirring unrest in both of our kingdoms, and we must act before it tears us apart."

Isla's eyes flickered with interest at the mention of the prophecy, but her expression remained guarded. "The prophecy," she repeated, her voice almost a whisper. "You and your father are not the only ones who fear it. In my kingdom, we too have felt its weight. There have been whispers—rumors of a hybrid king, of a being who will unite or destroy us all. But I assure you, Lord Aldrin, my people are not in the mood for peace talks. Empress Kaela's leadership is built on strength and survival. We do not trust easily, not even when the stakes are as high as they are now."

Aldrin felt the tension in her words. She was right to be cautious. The Glacial Dominion had been built on the backs of warriors, and Isla herself was no stranger to the harshness of survival. She was not a woman who would fall easily to diplomatic niceties.

"I understand," Aldrin said, choosing his words carefully. "But the time for war is not yet upon us. We still have a chance to prevent it. The hybrid king—the one spoken of in the prophecy—could be our salvation, or he could be the force that tears us all apart. I believe we have a common enemy, Lady Isla. If we do not unite, we will fall one by one."

Isla's lips pressed into a thin line, her gaze unwavering. She was clearly weighing his words. "And what do you propose, Lord Aldrin? How can Solara and the Dominion unite when our interests have long been at odds? We have our own threats to face, and our own people to protect."

Aldrin met her gaze, his resolve hardening. "I propose an alliance. We join forces, not just for ourselves, but for the future of all kingdoms. Together, we can face whatever is coming—and if the hybrid king is a threat, we will stand against him, side by side."

For a moment, Isla was silent. Her eyes searched Aldrin's face, as if trying to read his every thought. Then, slowly, she nodded.

"Perhaps," she said, her voice still laced with doubt, "but you must understand that peace is not easily won. There are factions within my kingdom—people who will see your presence here as a threat. You are not just representing your father, Aldrin. You are representing an entire kingdom, and in my lands, alliances are forged in blood."

As the meeting came to a close, Isla escorted Aldrin to a window overlooking the frigid landscape. The sight was breathtaking—glaciers stretching for miles, the cold beauty of the land stark and unforgiving. But there was a danger beneath that beauty. Aldrin could feel it in the air, the way the wind howled through the mountain passes like a warning. The hybrid king was coming, and whether they were ready or not, the kingdoms would soon be drawn into a battle they could not escape.

"Be careful," Isla warned, her voice soft but laden with meaning. "The prophecy may be more than just words. The hybrid king is not just a king. He is a force. And forces like that do not bow to anyone."

Aldrin nodded, the weight of her words settling deep within him. "I'll be ready," he said, though the doubt in his voice betrayed him.

As he left the palace that night, the cold seemed to press in on him from all sides. He had made progress with Isla, but the true challenge lay ahead. Empress Kaela's power was unyielding, and Isla's loyalty was tied to her kingdom—could he truly convince her that peace was the only path forward? Or would their differences tear the alliance apart before it even had a chance to begin?

As the first snow of the season began to fall softly from the sky, Aldrin couldn't shake the feeling that something was stirring beneath the surface—a force that neither he nor Isla were fully prepared to face.

The hybrid king was out there. And his rise would change everything.

The First Shifting Shadow

The journey south was quiet at first, save for the crunch of snow beneath Aldrin and Isla's horses. They traveled with a small escort through the frosty expanse of the Glacial Dominion, the cold air sharp against their skin. Though they moved with purpose, a weight hung between them—an unspoken tension born of the fragile trust they had forged.

Isla rode ahead, her eyes scanning the horizon. Despite her poise, Aldrin noticed her fingers lingering near the hilt of her dagger. She was always ready, always on edge—a habit honed from years of navigating the treacherous politics of her homeland. Aldrin couldn't help but admire her vigilance, though he wondered how long it would take for her to trust him.

The tension broke as they neared the edge of the Glacial Dominion, the snow beginning to thin. It was there, amidst the jagged cliffs, that they stumbled upon something they hadn't expected.

The first sign of trouble was the silence. No wind, no distant calls of birds, just an unnatural stillness that pressed in around them. Aldrin slowed his horse, his hand instinctively moving to his sword.

"Do you feel that?" Isla asked, her voice low.

He nodded. "Too quiet."

The group moved cautiously through the narrowing pass, the walls of ice and stone rising higher around them. The shadows grew longer as the sun dipped lower in the sky. Then, they saw it—a group of figures gathered in a clearing ahead. Cloaked and hooded, their forms were barely visible in the fading light.

Aldrin raised a hand, signaling the group to stop. "Stay here," he said, dismounting. "I'll approach."

Isla dismounted as well, drawing her dagger. "You're not going alone."

Together, they approached the clearing, their boots crunching softly on the frozen ground. As they drew closer, the figures became clearer. They were kneeling in a circle, chanting in a language that

Aldrin didn't recognize. In the center of the circle was a symbol carved into the ground—an intricate spiral surrounded by jagged lines, pulsing faintly with an unnatural glow.

"Shadows of the Abyss," Isla whispered, her voice filled with dread.

Aldrin glanced at her. "You know them?"

She nodded, her eyes fixed on the scene before them. "Fanatics. They worship the old gods, the ones cast out long ago. They've been quiet for years, but rumors say they've resurfaced, more dangerous than ever."

Before Aldrin could respond, one of the figures looked up. The hood fell back, revealing a pale, scarred face. The man's eyes glowed faintly, the same eerie light as the symbol on the ground. He smiled, a twisted, unnatural grin that sent a shiver down Aldrin's spine.

"Welcome," the man said, his voice unnervingly calm. "You're just in time."

The confrontation was swift and brutal. The cultists, armed with daggers and dark magic, attacked with ferocity. Aldrin and Isla fought side by side, their movements a seamless dance of steel and strategy. Despite their skill, the cultists seemed almost otherworldly, their wounds slowing them only momentarily.

As the battle raged, one of the cultists raised his arms, chanting in the strange language. The glowing symbol flared brighter, and the ground began to tremble. Aldrin lunged at the man, his sword slicing through the air, but it was too late. With a deafening roar, the symbol erupted in a burst of dark energy, sending him and Isla sprawling.

When the dust settled, the cultists were gone. The clearing was empty, save for the faint scorch marks where the symbol had been. Aldrin pushed himself to his feet, his body aching from the blast.

"Are you all right?" he asked, extending a hand to Isla.

She took it, her grip firm. "I'm fine. But this…" She gestured to the clearing. "This is no coincidence. The Shadows of the Abyss don't act without purpose."

Aldrin frowned. "What were they doing here?"

"Preparing," she said grimly. "For something—or someone."

Later that night, as they set up camp near the border of Solara, Aldrin couldn't shake the feeling of unease. The cultists' words echoed in his mind You're just in time. For what? He didn't have an answer, but he knew they hadn't seen the last of the Shadows.

His thoughts were interrupted by the arrival of a stranger. He appeared out of the darkness, his movements slow and deliberate. Clad in tattered robes, the man carried a staff adorned with strange carvings. His face was weathered, his eyes sharp and piercing.

"Travelers," the man said, his voice rough but steady. "You've encountered the shadows, haven't you?"

Aldrin rose to his feet, his hand on his sword. "Who are you?"

"A wanderer," the man replied. "Once a mage, long ago. I come from the Sandborn Lands, though I've walked far from home. I seek those who would stand against the coming storm."

Isla stepped forward, her expression wary. "What storm?"

The man's gaze seemed to pierce through her. "The one foretold. The hybrid king rises, and with him, the darkness. The Shadows of the Abyss serve a master greater than you can imagine—a force that will bring the mortal world to its knees."

Aldrin's grip on his sword tightened. "Do you know who the hybrid king is?"

The man smiled faintly. "I know many things, Lord of Solara. But the truth is a burden you must uncover yourself."

Before Aldrin could press him further, the man turned and began to walk away, his figure fading into the night.

"Wait!" Aldrin called, but the man didn't stop.

Isla placed a hand on his arm. "Let him go. If he wanted to tell us more, he would have."

As the camp settled into an uneasy silence, Aldrin couldn't shake the feeling that the stranger's words were a warning—and that the true battle was only just beginning.

Ravenor's Touch

Aldrin's days of quiet diplomacy came to an abrupt end on the road back to Solara. His party had just entered the warm, golden fields that marked the kingdom's outskirts when the ambush struck. The attack was swift, a blur of poisoned arrows and shadowclad assassins emerging from the underbrush.

Aldrin reacted instinctively, drawing his blade to deflect the first volley of arrows. His guards fell into formation around him, their shields raised, but the attackers were unlike anything they'd faced before. Their movements were unnaturally fast, their strikes precise and unrelenting.

Isla, still traveling with Aldrin's convoy, proved invaluable in the chaos. Armed with her twin daggers, she moved like a shadow herself, cutting down attackers with lethal efficiency.

Despite their skill, it was clear the attackers were after one target Aldrin. He narrowly avoided a dagger aimed for his heart, the blade grazing his arm as he spun to disarm his assailant. The attacker whispered chilling words before collapsing to the ground

"The hybrid king will rise. Solara will fall."

The aftermath left Aldrin visibly shaken. His party regrouped, battered but alive, and made haste to Solara's capital city, Sunspire. The attack was unlike anything Aldrin had faced before—not just an act of violence, but a calculated message.

King Alaric, Aldrin's father, received him in the grand hall of the Solar Keep, a fortress of marble and gold that reflected the warmth and prosperity of their kingdom. Though relieved his son was alive, Alaric's fury was evident.

"An attack on the crown prince is an attack on the kingdom itself," he declared, summoning his council. "We will not let this go unanswered."

Alaric ordered an immediate investigation into the ambush, but Aldrin's mind was already racing. The cultist's dying words haunted him. *The hybrid king will rise. Solara will fall.*

Later that evening, Aldrin sought the counsel of Varun, the kingdom's trusted strategist. Varun had been a close advisor to the royal family for decades, despite his physical disability. Bound to a chair of intricately carved wood and brass, Varun was often underestimated by those who didn't know him. But his piercing eyes and sharp mind left no doubt of his capabilities.

Varun greeted Aldrin in his chambers, which were lined with maps, scrolls, and relics from Solara's history. The strategist listened carefully as Aldrin recounted the attack, his weathered hands steepled in thought.

"The Shadows of the Abyss," Varun said at last. "Their reach grows bolder by the day. This attack wasn't random—it was a message."

Aldrin frowned. "A message from whom? The hybrid king? Ravenor?"

Varun's expression darkened. "Ravenor's name has been whispered in the shadows for years, long before your time, Aldrin. The cultists believe he is their savior—a harbinger of a new age. Whether this 'hybrid king' they speak of is real or a myth, it doesn't matter. What matters is their belief in him."

Varun wheeled himself to a nearby map, gesturing to the kingdoms surrounding Solara. "The cult's influence isn't confined to the wilderness. They've been infiltrating courts, stirring unrest, and orchestrating chaos for decades, perhaps longer. The attack on you is only the beginning."

Aldrin felt the weight of Varun's words settle heavily on his shoulders. "How do we fight an enemy that hides in the shadows?"

Varun turned to him, his voice steady. "By outthinking them. Strength alone won't win this battle. You must be cunning, patient, and unyielding. And you must trust those who stand with you, even if alliances seem fragile."

The words resonated with Aldrin. Despite his initial doubts, he was beginning to see Varun not just as an advisor, but as a mentor—someone who could guide him through the trials ahead.

The attack on Aldrin caused ripples throughout the kingdom. The court was thrown into disarray, with factions arguing over how to respond. Some called for retaliation against neighboring kingdoms, while others urged caution. The tension threatened to tear the court apart, and Aldrin found himself caught in the middle.

In the midst of this chaos, Isla approached him with a proposal.

"Your enemies are hiding in plain sight," she said, her tone firm. "If you want to root them out, you'll need someone who knows how to move in the shadows. Let me help."

Though hesitant, Aldrin agreed. Isla's knowledge of covert operations and her pragmatic approach were assets he couldn't afford to ignore. Together, they began to uncover disturbing truths—nobles within Solara who had secretly aligned with the cult, trade routes used to smuggle weapons, and whispers of an ancient artifact said to be the key to Ravenor's return.

As Aldrin delved deeper into the conspiracy, the threads began to lead back to a single, chilling conclusion the cult had been manipulating the kingdoms for generations. Their goal wasn't just chaos—it was domination, achieved through the rise of the hybrid king.

Varun, ever the voice of reason, cautioned Aldrin against rushing into action. "The enemy thrives on fear and division. If you act without a plan, you'll play directly into their hands."

But Aldrin's resolve was firm. The attack had solidified his determination to protect his kingdom, no matter the cost. As he prepared to confront the growing threat, he couldn't shake the feeling that the cult's shadow extended far beyond what they had uncovered.

In the depths of his mind, a question lingered Was the hybrid king already among them?

And somewhere, in the dark recesses of the world, Ravenor watched, his influence spreading like a disease. Though he had yet to reveal himself, his presence was palpable, a chilling reminder that the true battle was only beginning.

A Kingdom Divided

The Solar Keep, bathed in the amber glow of the setting sun, seemed more imposing than ever to Aldrin. Its golden spires were symbols of Solara's strength and unity, but inside its marble halls, tension simmered like a brewing storm. The council chamber was alive with heated arguments as nobles, generals, and advisors debated the kingdom's next move.

King Alaric sat at the head of the long table, his features lined with both authority and weariness. Despite his commanding presence, Aldrin noticed the subtle signs of a ruler burdened by the weight of his choices.

"We cannot sit idle while the Glacial Dominion strengthens its forces!" barked Lord Reddan, a fiery noble from the southern reaches of Solara. "The prophecy is clear—a great threat looms. We must strike first to ensure our survival!"

"And risk plunging the entire world into war?" countered Lady Elira, one of the few voices of reason in the court. "This prophecy is being used as an excuse to sow fear and chaos. Diplomacy is the answer, not bloodshed."

Aldrin listened in silence, his gaze shifting between the faces of the council. His father's expression was unreadable, but Aldrin could sense his inner turmoil. When the arguments reached a crescendo, King Alaric raised his hand, commanding silence.

"The safety of Solara must come first," he said, his voice measured. "But we will not act recklessly. We will investigate these threats and ensure our position is secure before making any decisions about war."

Though the king's words were meant to calm the room, Aldrin could see that they satisfied no one. The council was divided, and the kingdom itself seemed to be following suit.

Later that evening, Aldrin sought out Varun in his chambers. The strategist, as always, was surrounded by maps and scrolls, his sharp mind focused on deciphering the threads of chaos.

"The court is falling apart," Aldrin said, pacing the room. "Everyone has their own agenda, and no one seems to care about the bigger picture."

Varun looked up from his work, his expression calm but thoughtful. "The prophecy has shaken the foundations of this kingdom—and others as well. Fear is a powerful weapon, Aldrin. Ravenor knows this better than anyone."

Aldrin frowned. "Do you think he's behind the division in the court?"

"I have no doubt," Varun replied. "But his influence is subtle. He thrives in the shadows, sowing discord and mistrust. The question is not whether he's involved, but how far his reach extends."

As the court's debates raged on, Aldrin found himself drawn to the villages on the outskirts of Solara. Reports of strange occurrences had begun to surface—cattle slaughtered without explanation, children waking from nightmares with cryptic words on their lips, and shadowy figures seen lurking in the forests at night.

It was during one such visit that Aldrin encountered the first tangible sign of Ravenor's influence. He and his guards were investigating a burnedout village when they discovered the charred remains of a symbol etched into the ground—the same spiral surrounded by jagged lines that he had seen during the ambush in the Glacial Dominion.

The air around the symbol felt heavy, almost suffocating. Aldrin knelt beside it, his fingers brushing the scorched earth. A faint whisper reached his ears, too soft to make out but chilling nonetheless.

"Ravenor's mark," said one of the guards, his voice trembling.

Aldrin rose, his jaw set. "Whatever he's planning, it's escalating. We need answers."

The strangeness continued to grow. Creatures not native to Solara began appearing—serpentine beasts with glistening scales, their eyes glowing with an unnatural light, and massive birds with razorsharp talons that attacked travelers without provocation. Rumors spread like wildfire, and fear gripped the hearts of Solara's people.

In the capital, the court's divisions deepened. Lord Reddan and his faction pressed harder for war, while Lady Elira and her allies urged caution. Aldrin, caught in the middle, began to see the cracks in his father's rule. King Alaric was a strong leader, but his reliance on tradition and his reluctance to adapt to the changing world left him vulnerable.

Aldrin confided in Isla, who had remained in Solara to assist with the investigation. "I'm beginning to wonder if the prophecy is more than just a warning," he said. "What if it's a selffulfilling cycle? What if our fear of the hybrid king is the very thing that will bring him into power?"

Isla's expression was unreadable. "Prophecies are dangerous," she said. "They can manipulate even the wisest of rulers. But you're right to question them. Blindly following—or fearing—a prophecy is a sure path to destruction."

The tension reached a breaking point when an assassin was caught attempting to infiltrate the Solar Keep. Under interrogation, the assassin revealed chilling details he was a member of the Shadows of the Abyss, sent to sow discord and weaken Solara from within.

But it was his final words that sent a shiver down Aldrin's spine "The hybrid king is already here. You just don't see him yet."

The revelation left the court in turmoil. Accusations flew, with nobles turning on one another, each suspecting the other of collusion with the cult. Aldrin realized that Ravenor's plan was working—fear and mistrust were tearing Solara apart from the inside.

As Aldrin grappled with the growing chaos, he began to piece together a troubling pattern. The strange creatures, the attacks on villages, the infiltration of the court—everything pointed to one conclusion Ravenor's influence wasn't just spreading. It was being directed, as though he were testing the kingdom's defenses, preparing for something far greater.

In the quiet hours of the night, Aldrin stood on the battlements of the Solar Keep, gazing out at the horizon. The stars above were brilliant, but the darkness below felt allencompassing.

He couldn't shake the feeling that Ravenor was watching, his presence an invisible weight pressing down on the world. And though Aldrin didn't know it yet, the decisions he would make in the coming days would shape the fate of not just Solara, but all the kingdoms of the Earth.

The Unseen War

The air in the Solar Keep grew heavy with the tension of unspoken truths. The prophecy of the hybrid king had become a rallying cry for some and a curse for others. Throughout Solara, whispers of treachery and ambition spread like wildfire, and the onceunified kingdom teetered on the brink of chaos.

In the royal court, King Alaric summoned the high council for an emergency meeting. The reports from the Glacial Dominion and the Sandborn Lands painted a grim picture strange alliances were forming, skirmishes had erupted on shared borders, and rumors of the cult's growing power were no longer deniable.

"Do you not see?" thundered Lord Reddan, slamming his fist on the table. "This prophecy is not a warning—it is a call to action! If we do not act now, Solara will be swallowed whole by the darkness."

Lady Elira, standing firm in the face of the mounting hysteria, countered with measured resolve. "If we allow fear to dictate our actions, we will become the very monsters we seek to fight. Solara cannot survive a war on all fronts."

Aldrin watched the argument with growing unease. The lines between allies and enemies blurred further with every passing moment, and he could feel the kingdom's foundation cracking beneath the weight of their decisions.

Outside the court, Aldrin sought refuge in the quiet counsel of Varun. The old strategist was pouring over maps of Solara and the surrounding kingdoms, his keen mind searching for patterns in the chaos.

"The war has already begun, hasn't it?" Aldrin asked, breaking the silence.

Varun nodded, his gaze never leaving the parchment. "Not in the way you imagine. This is a war of shadows, Aldrin—a war of whispers and subterfuge. Ravenor's cult isn't seeking to destroy us outright. They're tearing us apart from within, one thread at a time."

Aldrin frowned. "Then how do we fight an enemy we can't see?"

Varun met his gaze, his voice heavy with meaning. "By learning to see what others cannot. The answers are there, hidden in the patterns of history, in the cracks of power. You must become the bridge between the known and the unknown."

Determined to uncover the truth, Aldrin and Isla set out on a dangerous mission to the Sandborn Lands, where they believe the cult's influence runs deepest. The journey is perilous, marked by sandstorms that strip the land bare and treacherous encounters with the hybrid creatures that Ravenor's followers have unleashed upon the world.

The Sandborn Lands, a kingdom of endless dunes and shifting sands, is a stark contrast to the glacial beauty of Isla's home. Its ruler, the enigmatic Sultan Idrak, presides over a realm where survival is an art form, and every grain of sand seems to whisper ancient secrets. Beneath the sands lie vast underground caverns filled with shimmering crystals, remnants of a longforgotten age of magic.

Aldrin and Isla infiltrate the bustling markets of the Sandborn capital, disguised as merchants. They uncover whispers of a secret gathering—a congregation of Ravenor's followers preparing for a ritual that will bring their dark master closer to the mortal realm.

Meanwhile, back in Solara, King Alaric faces rebellion from within. Nobles dissatisfied with his cautious approach begin conspiring against him, and the court becomes a battlefield of deceit. Varun works tirelessly to keep the kingdom from fracturing entirely, using his sharp intellect to outmaneuver the rebellious factions.

The situation reaches a boiling point when an envoy from the Glacial Dominion arrives with an ultimatum Solara must either ally with them against the Sandborn Lands or be seen as an enemy. The pressure mounts on King Alaric, whose health begins to falter under the strain.

In the Sandborn Lands, Aldrin and Isla infiltrate the cult's gathering, witnessing a ritual that chills them to their core. The cultists chant Ravenor's name, their voices merging into a single, haunting melody. The ground trembles as a figure steps forward—a child marked with the spiral of the hybrid king.

Aldrin's heart pounds as the implications sink in. The hybrid king is not some distant figure or future threat. He is here, now, and Ravenor's cult is preparing him to fulfill the prophecy.

As the ritual reaches its climax, Aldrin and Isla are discovered. A fierce battle ensues, and though they manage to escape, the cost is high. Aldrin is wounded, both physically and emotionally, as the weight of what he has seen threatens to crush him.

Returning to Solara, Aldrin confronts his father, demanding that the kingdom take action. But King Alaric, weakened by both illness and indecision, refuses to risk open war without proof that Solara can win.

Frustrated and disillusioned, Aldrin realizes that the fight against Ravenor will not be won in courtrooms or battlefields. It is a war of individuals, of choices made in the face of overwhelming darkness.

In the closing moments of the book, Aldrin stands on the battlements of the Solar Keep, watching the horizon. He knows that the hybrid king is real, that Ravenor's cult is closer to their goal than anyone had feared, and that the world is on the brink of irreversible change.

As the stars fade and dawn breaks, Aldrin makes a vow—to fight for the world, even if it means defying everything he once believed in. The unseen war has begun, and the embers of dominion are about to ignite into an inferno.

Book The Shattered Tides

A Storm Rising

The story opens in the Kingdom of Tides, a dazzling coastal realm famed for its sprawling harbor cities, intricate floating markets, and unmatched naval dominance. Azurehaven, the kingdom's capital, stands as a shimmering testament to its prosperity—a city of pearlescent towers, winding canals, and bustling trade ports. Beneath the glittering waves, however, lies a secret long forgotten the submerged ruins of an ancient civilization that once thrived by worshiping a formidable sea god known as Thalzor.

On a moonless night, far from Azurehaven's warm lights, a storm brews unnaturally fast. The Shadows of the Abyss, Ravenor's dark cult, gather in the depths of a secluded cove. Hooded figures chant in an arcane language, their words carried by the rising winds. A black altar, adorned with relics retrieved from the submerged ruins, pulses with unholy energy as the cult completes their ritual.

As the final chant echoes, the ocean boils, and an ominous silence falls. Moments later, the waters erupt with monstrous force. Massive storms spiral into existence, tearing apart ships and threatening coastal towns. From the deep, strange creatures, part fish and part nightmare, begin surfacing, haunting fishing villages and trade routes. Whispers spread among the terrified populace—Thalzor, the longdormant sea god, is awakening, and his wrath will drown the unworthy.

At the center of this rising chaos is Marea, a brilliant and charismatic leader of the Shadows of the Abyss. Marea is enigmatic and devout, claiming to have unlocked the secrets of the hybrid king from ancient texts hidden in the ruins. She preaches that the sea god will spare only those who submit to the hybrid king, the prophesied savior—or destroyer—of the world.

As the storms worsen and Marea's cult grows in influence, the Kingdom of Tides begins to splinter. Noble houses and merchants, desperate to protect their wealth and families, are divided in their allegiances. Some align with Queen Seris, the proud and strategic ruler of the kingdom, who refuses to bow to Ravenor's forces. Others, seduced by Marea's promises of salvation, join her cause, adding to the kingdom's unrest.

The closes with a haunting scene Marea stands atop the ruins, staring into the tumultuous waters. "The tides are rising," she whispers, her voice echoing unnaturally. In the depths below, something stirs—vast, ancient, and unstoppable. The leviathan is waking, and with it, the world will change forever.

The Summons

The morning sun rises over Solara's capital, its golden rays bouncing off the spires of the Citadel of Light, the heart of the kingdom. Aldrin, weighed down by the bitter memories of the Glacial Dominion and the everlooming specter of Ravenor, finds solace in the quiet company of Varun. Despite his physical disability, Varun remains a cornerstone of wisdom for Aldrin, offering sharp insights and a steadying presence. In a dimly lit study, Aldrin shares his growing unease about the Shadows of the Abyss and their unsettling reach.

"They are not just infiltrating kingdoms," Aldrin says. "They are unraveling the fabric of trust itself."

Varun listens, his gaze piercing. "Ravenor thrives in chaos. If you hesitate, chaos will swallow you."

Before Aldrin can delve deeper into his thoughts, a royal messenger interrupts, summoning him to the throne room. There, King Alaric, Aldrin's father, presides over an urgent council meeting. Maps are spread across a grand table, and the air is thick with tension.

Alaric's voice booms. "The Kingdom of Tides is crumbling. Their ports are in chaos, their trade routes strangled. Solara depends on those routes for grain, gems, and weapons. If we don't act, our economy will falter—and our enemies will seize the advantage."

Aldrin is tasked with traveling to the Kingdom of Tides to secure an alliance with Queen Seris. It's a dangerous mission, but Aldrin sees it as an opportunity to uncover more about Ravenor's schemes. Alaric insists on haste, warning that Solara cannot afford another destabilized ally.

As preparations begin, Aldrin is joined by Isla, who has grown more wary but remains steadfast in her resolve to see Ravenor's threat extinguished. To navigate the treacherous waters of the Sea of Specters, they enlist Captain Kael, a grizzled sailor with a shadowed past and a reputation for surviving impossible odds. Kael, rough around the edges but fiercely loyal, is their best chance of reaching the Kingdom of Tides safely.

Their journey begins with a foreboding departure. The Sea of Specters, infamous for its ghostly mists and rumored shipwrecks, lies ahead. As their ship vanishes into the horizon, Varun watches from the Citadel's balcony, murmuring to himself, "The tides will test him—more than he knows."

The closes with Aldrin aboard the ship, staring out at the vast expanse of ocean. His thoughts are a whirlwind of doubt and determination. Beneath the deck, Kael sharpens a dagger while Isla studies a tattered map, her brow furrowed. Overhead, storm clouds begin to gather. The journey to the Kingdom of Tides has begun, and with it, the first steps toward an unforeseen reckoning.

The Pearl Throne

The ship crests the last wave as Azurehaven, the capital of the Kingdom of Tides, comes into view. Aldrin, Isla, and Captain Kael stand at the prow, taking in the breathtaking sight. The city sprawls across a vast bay, its glittering waters crisscrossed by gondolas and trading ships. Floating markets bob gently on the waves, their vibrant canopies bursting with exotic goods—pearls, spices, and intricate seashell carvings. Towering sea walls encircle the city, built to withstand both the tide and invaders, while the central palace, the Pearl Throne, gleams in the sunlight, its spires shaped like coral reefs.

But as they dock, the city's charm gives way to an undercurrent of tension. The bustling streets are lined with merchants whose voices carry a note of desperation, performers whose smiles seem forced, and guards whose eyes dart nervously toward the harbor. Noble families gather in shadowed alcoves, speaking in hushed tones about rebellion and doom. Whispers of the Shadows of the Abyss and sightings of hybrid sea creatures—the Children of the Deep—have left the people paralyzed with fear.

The group is escorted to the Pearl Throne, a palace as imposing as it is beautiful. The throne room itself is a marvel—its walls are carved from shimmering white stone, and the floor is a mosaic of the kingdom's history, depicting victories at sea and trade routes carved across the globe. The air is heavy with the salt of the ocean and the weight of expectation.

Queen Seris, seated on a throne shaped like a breaking wave, greets Aldrin with a guarded expression. Her presence is commanding; her emeraldgreen armor glints under the light, and her dark hair is adorned with small pearls. She listens intently as Aldrin introduces himself and explains his mission.

Seris reveals the extent of her kingdom's plight. Many of her court members, frustrated by her resistance to Marea's growing cult, have turned against her. Marea preaches salvation through submission to the hybrid king and the awakening of Thalzor, the ancient sea god. This has caused a rift among the noble houses, with some secretly aligning with Marea to secure power should the cult succeed.

"Her words are poison," Seris says, her voice sharp with anger. "She twists the prophecy to sow chaos, and my kingdom is drowning in its wake."

Aldrin learns that Marea's cult has grown bolder, conducting rituals near coastal villages and summoning the Children of the Deep, terrifying hybrids of man and sea creature. These creatures raid settlements, leaving destruction in their wake and fueling the belief that Thalzor's wrath is imminent.

Determined to help, Aldrin proposes a strategy to unify the noble houses against the cult. Seris, though impressed by his resolve, warns him that the path will be perilous. The court's loyalty is fractured, and the cult's grip extends even into her inner circle.

As night falls, Aldrin, Isla, and Kael retire to their quarters within the palace. While Kael sharpens his blades and Isla studies maps of the region, Aldrin gazes out at the moonlit harbor. He cannot shake the feeling that something ancient and malevolent is watching from beneath the waves.

The closes with a haunting scene deep in the ocean, Marea stands on a jagged altar, leading a ritual. Around her, the Shadows of the Abyss chant in unison. The water stirs, and glowing eyes emerge from the darkness. The Children of the Deep bow to her, their guttural voices echoing her words

"The tide will claim the unworthy, and Thalzor shall rise."

Beneath the Waves

The morning sun glints off the rippling waters as Eirik, a brighteyed scholar from Azurehaven, joins Aldrin and Isla. Eirik is a man of contradictions—eager yet cautious, idealistic yet haunted by the secrets of the sea. "The ruins hold answers," he says as he unfurls a faded map of the bay. "But answers come with their own dangers."

Eirik guides them to a remote part of the bay where jagged rocks rise from the waves like the teeth of a great beast. Beneath these rocks lie the ruins of an ancient civilization, swallowed by the ocean centuries ago. With a small crew and a vessel equipped for diving, the group ventures into the depths.

As they descend into the shimmering blue, the water grows colder, the light dimmer. The ruins come into view—crumbled towers encrusted with coral, arches draped in seaweed, and statues eroded by time. Among the debris, intricate carvings cover the walls of a central temple. The group's torches reveal a haunting story

The carvings depict a mortal figure kneeling before a colossal sea god. The god's form is ambiguous, its body shifting between human and marine features, but its presence exudes power. The figure rises, transformed—a hybrid king wielding a trident that commands both the waves and the creatures of the deep. The imagery shifts to chaos as kingdoms are shown collapsing under tidal waves and storms.

"This... this is the prophecy," Isla whispers, her voice trembling. "The hybrid king was chosen by the sea god, but at what cost?"

Eirik, wideeyed, adds, "These ruins don't just speak of the past—they are a warning. If Thalzor is awakened, history may repeat itself."

Their exploration takes a dire turn when eerie clicking sounds echo through the water. Shadows dart between the ruins, and before they can react, the Children of the Deep strike. These creatures, their bodies twisted amalgamations of human and marine anatomy, move with unnatural speed. Their claws gleam, and their eyes glow with an unholy light.

The group fights desperately, Aldrin wielding a blade while Isla fires arrows from her compact crossbow. Eirik, untrained in combat, scrambles to shield himself. Despite their efforts, the Children of the Deep overwhelm them, forcing a retreat.

A sudden burst of light erupts from Isla's enchanted torch, disorienting the creatures just long enough for the group to escape to their vessel. As they surface, gasping for air, Aldrin's mind races. The carvings, the prophecy, the ambush—all confirm that Ravenor's cult is closer to their goal than anyone suspected.

The ends with the group back in Azurehaven, battered but alive. Aldrin and Isla recount their findings to Queen Seris, whose face pales at the mention of the hybrid king. Meanwhile, in the shadows of the palace, a noble secretly aligned with Marea overhears their discussion and slips away into the night.

Far beneath the waves, Marea watches from her ritual site, her expression serene. "They've seen the truth," she murmurs. "Now, let them witness the storm."

Treachery Unveiled

The air in Azurehaven's Pearl Throne palace is heavy with tension. Aldrin, Isla, and Eirik stand by as Queen Seris holds court, attempting to calm the nobles, who bicker over rumors of rebellion and the growing influence of Marea. The voices grow louder, accusations flying like arrows, until a sudden commotion silences the room.

A hooded figure, blending with the palace staff, lunges toward Seris with a concealed blade. Chaos erupts as guards clash with the assassin, but it's Isla's quick aim and Aldrin's sword that neutralize the attacker. The assassin, gravely injured, gasps out a final declaration

"For the hybrid king! For Thalzor!"

The failed attempt sends shockwaves through the court, but worse follows. That evening, during an emergency meeting of the nobles, Lord Maros, a respected yet ambitious figure, declares his allegiance to Marea. His words drip with fervor as he accuses Seris of defying the sea god's will and jeopardizing the kingdom's salvation.

"You deny the prophecy," Maros bellows, standing atop the council table. "But the signs are clear—the storms, the creatures, the rising tides. Thalzor will return, and only those who embrace his chosen king will survive."

His proclamation divides the room. Some nobles murmur agreement, others call for his immediate execution, but Seris, her composure razorsharp, silences them with a single command.

"Arrest him," she orders, her voice cutting through the noise. But as the guards advance, Maros laughs, a chilling sound.

"You think this ends with me?" he taunts. "The kingdom is already ours."

The guards hesitate, some lowering their weapons—proof that Marea's influence has infiltrated even Seris's inner circle. Maros escapes amidst the confusion, retreating into the city to join Marea's growing faction.

In the days that follow, the city is plunged into turmoil. News of Maros's defection emboldens Marea's supporters, who take to the streets in defiance of Seris's rule. Whispers of salvation through the hybrid king spread like wildfire, and Seris faces mounting pressure from her dwindling allies.

Determined to act, Aldrin pleads with Seris to consider an alliance with Solara, even if only temporary. At first, she resists—her pride as queen and her kingdom's history of independence make the idea of relying on Solara unthinkable. But as reports of Marea's forces overtaking nearby villages pour in, she grudgingly agrees.

"This alliance," she warns Aldrin, "is born of necessity, not trust. I will not kneel to Solara—or anyone else."

Meanwhile, Ravenor's presence looms larger, though he remains unseen. Marea's speeches grow more impassioned, her promises of salvation laced with an eerie conviction. She invokes Ravenor's name as a savior and the hybrid king as his chosen one, further deepening the divisions within the kingdom.

As the ends, Aldrin, Isla, and Eirik prepare to leave Azurehaven to investigate reports of Marea's cult gathering at an ancient coastal temple. Seris stands at the palace gates, watching them depart. Her expression is stoic, but a flicker of doubt crosses her face.

Far away, in a hidden cove, Marea kneels before an altar. The sea swirls unnaturally around her as she whispers, "Soon, my king. Soon you shall rise, and all will bow before the tide."

The Leviathan Awakens

The skies over Azurehaven darken as Marea's cult gathers along the jagged cliffs of the Temple of Tides, an ancient structure carved into the seaside rock. Chanting fills the air, their voices weaving a sinister melody with the crashing waves below. At the heart of the ritual, Marea, draped in ceremonial robes and holding the Trident of Thalzor, completes the final incantation.

From the depths of the ocean, a low rumble reverberates, growing into a deafening roar as the Leviathan, a massive sea monster bound by forgotten magic, rises. Its gargantuan form eclipses the horizon, its glowing eyes searing with fury. The beast's emergence causes tidal waves that batter Azurehaven's mighty sea walls, flooding its lower districts and sending citizens into panic.

Aldrin, Isla, Eirik, and Captain Kael race to the city's defense. Queen Seris rallies her navy, her voice cutting through the chaos as she commands her fleet to intercept the monster. But the Leviathan proves unstoppable, its sheer size and power overwhelming the ships and defenses.

Aldrin and Isla recall the relics they discovered in the underwater ruins—ancient devices imbued with protective magic. Alongside Eirik's knowledge of the ruins, they devise a plan to use these relics to weaken the Leviathan. However, activating the relics requires proximity to the beast, a nearsuicidal mission.

Kael, burdened by guilt over his shadowy past as a smuggler who once aided the cult unknowingly, volunteers for the most dangerous task. As Aldrin and Isla create a diversion using the relics, Kael pilots a small ship loaded with explosives toward the Leviathan, luring it away from the city.

In a moment of heroic sacrifice, Kael's ship collides with the Leviathan, triggering a massive explosion that sends the beast retreating into the depths. Azurehaven is saved—for now.

The victory comes at a heavy cost. The city lies in ruins, its navy decimated, and its people left shaken by the power of Ravenor's forces. Worse, Marea escapes amidst the chaos, retreating to the temple with artifacts stolen from the ruins. These artifacts, imbued with the sea god's power, will enable Ravenor's influence to grow even stronger.

As the closes, Aldrin stands on the battered shoreline, watching the distant horizon. The Leviathan's retreat does not feel like a victory—it feels like the calm before an even greater storm.

In a secret cove, Marea kneels once more before an altar, her hands gripping the stolen artifacts. "The Leviathan is but the first," she whispers. "Soon, the tide will drown the world, and the king will claim his throne."

The Shattered Tides

In the aftermath of the Leviathan's assault, Azurehaven stands in ruins. The onceproud coastal city, known for its opulence and bustling trade, now lies battered by waves and riddled with crumbled buildings. The shores are littered with debris, and the people of the Kingdom of

Tides are left to mourn the loss of loved ones, their homes, and their sense of security.

Queen Seris, though visibly shaken, remains steadfast. Her resolve is unbroken, though the weight of the defeat hangs heavy on her shoulders. The assassination attempts, the betrayal from within her court, and the rise of Marea have left deep scars on her kingdom. Yet, she vows to rebuild, starting with rallying her people to resist Marea's influence and protect the future of the kingdom. Seris, a natural leader, begins to focus on forging stronger alliances with neighboring kingdoms, particularly Solara. She understands that only a united front will stand a chance against the growing darkness.

However, the cost of survival is evident. Those who once stood by Seris's rule are now fractured, some siding with Marea's cult, believing in her prophecy and the return of the sea god. Tensions rise within the royal court as conflicting factions struggle for power. While Seris is determined to hold the kingdom together, it's clear that trust has been broken, and the foundation of the Kingdom of Tides is dangerously fragile.

Aldrin, having been a key player in the battle against the Leviathan, finds himself more burdened than ever. He returns to his quarters in the heart of the shattered kingdom, his thoughts weighed down by the aftermath of the battle and the growing threat of Ravenor's reach. The ancient prophecy of the hybrid king haunts him, as does the knowledge that Ravenor's influence stretches far beyond the Kingdom of Tides.

As he reflects on the carnage, Aldrin realizes that diplomacy alone will not be enough to unite the kingdoms. He has seen firsthand the corruption sown by Ravenor's cult—how Marea's vision of the hybrid king has manipulated the hearts of the people, and how Ravenor's dark magic has shattered the bonds between onceallied kingdoms. The belief in the prophecy of the hybrid king is spreading like wildfire, and Aldrin begins to fear that even the strongest alliances may not be enough to hold back the tide of destruction.

Alone in his thoughts, Aldrin ponders the impossible question Is there another way to stop Ravenor, or will they be forced into a war that will consume everything? The path forward is unclear, but the urgency to act grows with each passing day.

In the distance, the Shadows of the Abyss grow bolder. Marea's cult has not disappeared—they are regrouping, and the power of the artifacts she stole has only deepened Ravenor's grasp on the kingdoms. As the book nears its end, a messenger arrives from Solara, bringing word from King Alaric the time has come for Aldrin to take action and unite the kingdoms in an effort to confront Ravenor before it's too late.

But as Aldrin prepares to leave, a shadowy figure watches from the cliffs above Azurehaven. The figure is cloaked, but the unmistakable trident insignia of Marea is visible on their tunic. A storm brews in the distance, and Aldrin feels the weight of his choices. The future of the kingdoms rests in his hands, and every move he makes will bring him closer to the truth behind the hybrid king.

The final words of the linger in his mind "The tide is shifting. The world will be shattered."

Epilogue Ravenor's Shadow

The sun sets over a quiet, isolated cove, the deep blue of the ocean blending into the twilight sky. The sound of the waves crashing against jagged rocks is a stark contrast to the tense silence that lingers in the air. In the shadows of a small cave, Marea, cloaked in dark robes, stands before a hooded figure whose presence is both commanding and unsettling. The figure's face is obscured by a deep hood, but his aura of malevolence radiates through the very air.

Marea, her eyes filled with both ambition and fear, carefully places the stolen relics on the stone altar before her. These powerful artifacts, once held in secret places within the Kingdom of Tides, are now in her possession. Each one pulses with dark magic, a tangible connection to

Ravenor, whose influence stretches far and wide. She steps back, her hands trembling slightly as she speaks.

Marea "The time has come. The relics are in place. The prophecy will be fulfilled. The hybrid king is closer to being revealed than ever before. The kingdoms will not be able to withstand the storm that's coming."

The hooded figure nods, his voice a low, rumbling whisper that carries an unsettling power.

Emissary of Ravenor "The tides are turning, Marea. The hybrid king is the key to unlocking the world's true fate. When he arises, the kingdoms will bow before Ravenor. But until that moment, you must keep sowing discord. There is still much to be done before the final reckoning."

Marea nods, her eyes darkening with resolve. She looks down at the relics one last time before turning back to the emissary.

Marea "I will ensure that chaos reigns. The world will be reshaped in our image. The hybrid king will be our vessel."

The emissary steps forward, his hand outstretched, and Marea places the relics into his grasp. The moment their fingers touch, the air around them shivers with dark energy. The emissary smiles, a wicked grin barely visible beneath his hood.

Emissary of Ravenor "The world has already begun to change. The shadows of Ravenor will cover the kingdoms, and nothing will stand in their way."

With that, the emissary turns and vanishes into the darkness, leaving Marea alone with her thoughts. She watches the waves crashing violently on the shore, the power of the sea reflecting the chaos that is about to engulf the world. Her eyes narrow as she contemplates the future—one where the prophecy will finally come to fruition, and Ravenor will rule once more.

As the scene shifts, the narrative turns to Aldrin, standing on the high cliffs of Azurehaven, looking out over the turbulent sea. The winds whip around him, echoing the turmoil in his heart. The scars of the battle against the Leviathan still linger, but they are nothing compared to the weight of the coming war. The uneasy alliance with the Kingdom of Tides hangs in the balance, and Ravenor's cult grows bolder with each passing day.

Aldrin, though battleworn and weary, remains resolute. His mind is filled with plans, strategies, and a sense of duty that drives him forward. But deep down, he knows the truth the storm is far from over.

The hybrid king, a being of immense power, is closer to being revealed. And when that happens, the world will be forced to reckon with the terrifying prophecy that threatens everything.

As Aldrin gazes out at the horizon, the final words of the epilogue linger in the air "The tides of war have only just begun. Ravenor's shadow stretches long, and the kingdoms are on the brink of destruction."

The Shadow's Reach

The world is still reeling from the chaos unleashed by Marea and her cult in the Kingdom of Tides. Though the Leviathan has been subdued, the kingdom lies fractured, struggling to rebuild after the massive destruction caused by the giant sea creature and the treachery of those who sided with the cult. Coastal cities remain in ruin, and many citizens still live in fear of the hybrid creatures that continue to haunt the shores.

Across the seas, in the distant Eclipsed Lands, a new storm is brewing, one more terrifying than anything that has come before. The ancient prophecy of the hybrid king grows clearer, inching ever closer to fulfillment. Whispers of the king's return grow louder, echoing in dark corners of the world, unsettling the very foundations of the kingdoms.

In the shadows, a mysterious figure known only as the Harbinger begins to weave his influence. Cloaked in secrecy, the Harbinger has managed to gather dark power from across the lands, drawing followers to his cause. His true identity is unknown, but his presence is undeniable. His movements are subtle, but his reach extends far beyond the shores of any single kingdom. As his influence grows, so does the fear that the hybrid king will soon come into full power, heralding a time of upheaval and destruction.

The eclipse of the sun, a longfeared event, is drawing near. According to the prophecies, this eclipse will mark the moment when the hybrid king is fully awakened. The very skies themselves will be darkened as the king's power surges across the world, and the future will be irrevocably altered. The leaders of the kingdoms are unaware of the impending disaster, blinded by their own ambitions and struggles. They are illprepared for the reckoning that approaches, and the coming war will test the limits of their power and their resolve.

The Summons

Aldrin returned to the capital of Solara, his mind heavy with the aftermath of the devastating events in the Kingdom of Tides. The echoes of the Leviathan's roar and the growing influence of Marea's cult still haunted him. The delicate balance between kingdoms was crumbling, and Aldrin felt the weight of his decisions pressing down on him. In the quiet of his chambers, he confided in Varun, his disabled mentor who had been his guide through many of life's challenges.

Varun, though physically frail, was a sage with a sharp mind and a deep understanding of the forces that shaped the world. He had watched Aldrin grow from a headstrong young prince into a leader, but even Varun could see the darkness that was creeping across the lands.

The whispers of Ravenor's cult were growing louder, and the shadow of the hybrid king threatened to engulf them all. Yet, Varun's advice remained steady Aldrin had to continue moving forward, even in the face of unknown dangers.

Before Aldrin could absorb Varun's counsel, a summons from King Alaric, his father, arrived. The king had urgent orders for Aldrin he was to travel to the Eclipsed Lands, a mysterious and largely unexplored region at the edge of the known world. Rumors had reached Solara of dark forces gathering there, forces that could be tied to Ravenor's cult and the prophecy of the hybrid king.

The Eclipsed Lands, known for their treacherous seas and endless storms, had always been shrouded in mystery. The region's people were known for their isolationist ways, and little was known about their rulers. However, recent reports suggested that something far darker was unfolding within its borders.

While the Kingdom of Tides still struggled to recover, and the Solara trade routes were becoming increasingly perilous, Aldrin had no choice but to heed his father's summons. He was torn between his duty to Solara and his fear of what lay beyond the borders of his kingdom. As he prepared to leave, a messenger arrived with more troubling news Captain Kael, the hardened sailor who had become a close ally during the crisis in Tides, had been sent ahead to scout the Eclipsed Lands—but he had not reported back in weeks.

The situation was dire. Aldrin could not ignore the possibility that something had happened to Kael, and with that, the threat in the Eclipsed Lands could be more immediate than they had anticipated.

Determined to uncover the truth, Aldrin gathered his trusted ally Isla, the diplomat from the Glacial Dominion, and set off on his journey. Accompanying them were Captain Kael's old crew, now under the command of Joren, a fiercely loyal and secretive sailor who had served alongside Kael for many years. Joren's expertise in navigating the

Sea of Specters—the treacherous and ghostly waters that separated the kingdoms from the Eclipsed Lands—would prove invaluable.

Aldrin's mission was clear find Kael, investigate the growing dark forces in the Eclipsed Lands, and stop another war from breaking out. But deep inside, he feared that what they would find would be far worse than they could imagine. As the ship sailed towards the unknown, Aldrin couldn't shake the feeling that the darkness was already reaching out, its tendrils pulling them into a web of chaos from which there would be no escape.

The Search for Kael

The journey to the Eclipsed Lands was a treacherous one from the start. As the ship sailed deeper into the Sea of Specters, the crew was met with increasingly violent storms that seemed to rise out of nowhere. The Sea of Specters, infamous for its unpredictable winds and eerie fog, had earned its name from sailors who spoke of ghostly apparitions and unnatural phenomena that haunted its waters. Yet, Aldrin and his crew had no choice but to press on. They could not afford to turn back. Kael, their former ally, was out there somewhere, and they had to find him.

As they ventured deeper into the storm, the winds howled like angry spirits, and the sea churned beneath them with terrifying force. Lightning flashed, illuminating the jagged waves, while thunder boomed in the heavens. The ship rocked violently, and Aldrin found himself gripping the rail, struggling to maintain his balance. The oncesturdy vessel creaked and groaned under the relentless battering of the storm. The crew worked together with practiced precision, but the sea seemed intent on devouring them whole.

Then, as if the storm itself had turned against them, a massive wave crashed over the deck, sending several crew members into the water. The ship was torn in two, its sails shredded by the violent wind.

Aldrin's heart pounded as he saw Isla, fighting to stay upright, and the crew scrambling to regain control. Amidst the chaos, Aldrin heard the unmistakable sound of splintering wood. The ship's mast snapped, and the vessel was swallowed by the storm.

By sheer luck and determination, Aldrin, Isla, and the remaining crew managed to survive the shipwreck. After hours of struggling against the storm and the crashing waves, they finally made landfall on a mysterious island. It was uncharted and strange, with rocky cliffs rising sharply from the sea and dense jungles that seemed to pulse with an unnatural energy.

The island was silent, its atmosphere heavy with an eerie sense of ancient power. Aldrin led the group inland, cautiously searching for any sign of Kael. They soon discovered ruins that hinted at a longlost civilization—strange symbols carved into the stone, walls covered with faded murals depicting powerful mages and gods, and remnants of structures that suggested this place had once been the center of great magical power.

But despite their best efforts, there was no sign of Kael. The only clue left behind was a single, bloodstained map found near the ruins. The map was old, its edges frayed and weathered, but it marked a specific location deep within the Eclipsed Lands. The place marked on the map was a point where the eclipse was predicted to be strongest—a location that seemed to hold deep significance in the growing storm of darkness.

As Aldrin examined the map, a sense of foreboding settled over him. Whatever had transpired here, it was linked to the ancient forces that Ravenor's cult sought to awaken. But why had Kael come here? And what had he found before disappearing?

Isla, ever the pragmatist, was growing increasingly wary of their mission. "This island, the storm, the ruins—none of it makes sense," she said, her voice tinged with unease. "We need to be careful, Aldrin. We're walking into something far darker than we could have imagined."

Her words resonated with Aldrin, who was starting to feel the weight of their journey. As the group sat around a fire that evening, the shadows dancing eerily in the flickering flames, Aldrin allowed himself a moment of vulnerability. His usual confidence had begun to crack under the pressure. He turned to Isla, his voice quieter than usual.

"I fear we may be too late, Isla. The world feels as though it's already slipping through our fingers. I thought I could stop this—find a way to hold it all together—but the more I learn, the more I feel we're being dragged toward a fate we can't escape."

Isla studied him for a long moment, her expression unreadable. She had always seen Aldrin as a symbol of hope, but even she could sense the growing despair in his voice. She knew his mind was torn, battling between the weight of the prophecy and his duty to protect his kingdom.

"We'll find Kael," Isla replied, her tone soft but resolute. "And we'll stop whatever is coming. We have to. For the sake of everything we've fought for."

Aldrin nodded, though the uncertainty in his heart remained. He knew Isla's words were meant to comfort him, but the shadows of doubt continued to loom large. With the bloodstained map in hand, they had no choice but to continue their journey into the heart of the Eclipsed Lands, where the eclipse—and whatever dark power it heralded—awaited.

The First Sign of the Harbinger

Aldrin and his crew ventured deeper into the heart of the Eclipsed Lands, their path obscured by thick, unwelcoming forests and the shadow of ancient mountains looming over them. The land itself seemed steeped in mystery, as though it had been forgotten by time. The people they encountered were reclusive, speaking in hushed tones and often turning away when Aldrin's group approached. A sense of paranoia gripped the land; the oncethriving villages were now reduced to quiet, desolate hamlets, and whispers of something dark in the distance kept the locals on edge.

As Aldrin navigated these troubled lands, it became evident that they were no longer just dealing with a simple political threat. The rumors of a mysterious figure known only as The Harbinger began to surface in their conversations. Villagers spoke of him in both fear and reverence. He was described as a man who could sway entire towns with a few words, a charismatic leader with a dark agenda. His followers were growing in number, and though his face remained unknown, his presence was felt everywhere. Some believed he was the true harbinger of the hybrid king, while others feared that his influence would soon plunge the world into darkness.

The figure of the Harbinger intrigued Aldrin. He couldn't help but sense that this man—whoever he was—was somehow tied to the growing unrest that threatened the kingdoms. His name had not yet reached the halls of Solara's court, but it was only a matter of time before his actions were felt across the seas.

In a secluded village, they met Eirik, a young and ambitious scholar with a passion for the forgotten histories of the Eclipsed Lands. Eirik had been researching the ancient civilizations that once called the Eclipsed Lands home. He was convinced that the stories and prophecies about the hybrid king were not merely folklore but were rooted in truth.

"They didn't just worship gods," Eirik explained, his eyes alight with excitement and dread. "They sought to control powers beyond their understanding—forces tied to the eclipse, powers that could shape the world. The hybrid king is real, Aldrin. And he is the key to unlocking something far more dangerous."

Eirik's discovery was both a revelation and a warning. He revealed ancient texts that described a time when the eclipse would come once again, bringing with it the awakening of the hybrid king. But it wasn't just a king—it was a force of nature, bound to an ancient entity of darkness, a being whose very presence could undo the balance of the world. The prophecy spoke of a time when this king would rise and bring a new world order, one that would bow to his power.

Before Aldrin could ask more, a cold, unsettling presence swept over the group. It came without warning, as though the land itself had grown hostile. From the shadows of the forest, a figure emerged—tall and cloaked, with glowing red eyes that seemed to pierce through the darkness. His very presence seemed to bend the air around him, a force of unnatural strength. He was not like any mortal man Aldrin had ever faced.

The figure moved with eerie speed, striking without warning. His movements were fluid, almost inhuman. Aldrin barely had time to draw his sword before the figure was upon them, his glowing eyes locking with Aldrin's as if sensing the uncertainty in his heart. With a speed that left the crew in shock, the figure swiped through their defenses, his strength overwhelming their combined efforts.

It was Isla who first shouted the command to retreat, pulling Aldrin and the others back. They barely managed to escape into the woods, their hearts pounding with fear and confusion. The figure remained behind, his eyes still glowing in the distance, as if daring them to face him again. He left them with a chilling message, one that echoed in Aldrin's mind long after they had retreated to safety

"The hybrid king is near. The world will bow to darkness."

The words sent a ripple of unease through Aldrin's group. The prophecy was no longer just a distant threat. It was real, and it was coming for them. The Harbinger was not just a name—it was a force gathering strength in the shadows, preparing to rise.

As they regrouped, Aldrin realized that their mission had just become far more dangerous than they could have imagined. They were not just searching for Kael anymore. They were hunting something far more elusive, something far more dangerous—an ancient power that, if unleashed, could change the fate of the world. And it was only a matter of time before the darkness would find them.

A Deadly Betrayal

The journey grew darker with each passing day as Aldrin's group ventured deeper into the heart of the Eclipsed Lands. The once vague whispers of a looming threat were now tangible, and the specter of the Harbinger seemed to follow their every move. But nothing could prepare Aldrin for the discovery they made in a coastal village on the edge of the lands—a discovery that would forever alter the course of their mission.

The small village was nearly deserted, the few remaining villagers wary and afraid. They spoke of strange men in the night and voices calling out from the sea, but they did little to help Aldrin and his crew. The village felt suffocating, like a place abandoned by hope. Yet, amid the quiet desolation, Aldrin found something he hadn't expected—a body.

It was Captain Kael.

The discovery hit Aldrin like a hammer to the chest. Kael, the grizzled sailor who had been a mentor of sorts, a companion who had fought by Aldrin's side in the Kingdom of Tides, was now dead. His body lay lifeless near the shore, cruelly battered by the harsh elements, but the wounds on his body told a different story—this was no accident or natural death.

Kael had been murdered.

The wounds were numerous, and each seemed deliberate—signs of a brutal ambush. His face was pale, his eyes lifeless, and his body had been left exposed as if to send a message. But there was something else that drew Aldrin's attention—a small, weathered letter, sealed with wax, tucked tightly into Kael's hand. With trembling fingers, Aldrin broke the seal and unfolded the letter. The words inside sent a chill down his spine.

The letter was from Kael, written in haste. He had discovered something that Aldrin had feared but couldn't fully grasp the true identity of the Harbinger.

"The Harbinger is no myth. He is the one who binds the eclipse to his will. The king the prophecy speaks of is not just a ruler—it is an ancient power, a force to remake the world." Kael's handwriting trembled as if the gravity of the revelation weighed on him too heavily.

"I've seen his face. His power grows with every passing day. The eclipse is his moment—his ascension. If I do not act now, it will be too late. He plans to summon the hybrid king during the eclipse. All will bow before him."

"I tried to stop him. But he's too powerful. I won't make it out alive. Aldrin, if you find this, know that everything we've been told has been a lie. The Harbinger is the key to this world's destruction. You must stop him."

Aldrin's hands trembled as he read the final words, his breath caught in his throat. Kael's suspicions had been right, but they had cost him his life. The letter confirmed what Aldrin had feared—the Harbinger was more than just a shadowy figure pulling the strings. He was the orchestrator of an ancient power, a force that sought to awaken the hybrid king, and with him, a reckoning that could destroy everything.

Aldrin stood there for a long moment, staring at the lifeless body of his former ally. His chest ached with grief, but there was no time to mourn. Kael's death was a grim confirmation of the danger they faced. The Harbinger's plan was in motion, and Kael had given his life in an attempt to stop it.

But the more Aldrin thought about the letter, the more questions arose. If the Harbinger was truly the key to the hybrid king's awakening, then how many others were involved in this dark conspiracy? What would the eclipse truly bring? And what price would Aldrin and his companions have to pay to stop it?

The questions felt overwhelming, and the weight of leadership grew heavier with each passing day. The path before him was no longer clear. The shadow of the Harbinger had grown too large to ignore, and Kael's death was a stark reminder that the cost of failure would be more than just lives—it would be the world itself.

As Aldrin looked out over the sea, his thoughts turned to the future. They had to keep moving forward. Kael's sacrifice would not be in vain. He had died fighting for something bigger than himself, and now Aldrin had no choice but to honor that sacrifice.

With a heavy heart, Aldrin turned to his crew, his voice barely a whisper.

"We continue. We find the Harbinger. And we stop him before it's too late."

The group, their faces grim but determined, nodded in agreement. The stakes had just become far higher than any of them could have imagined. With Kael's death, they had lost an ally, but gained a clearer understanding of the enemy they faced—a shadowy figure whose reach was growing by the day, and whose plan would soon come to fruition. The eclipse was fast approaching. And the world was running out of time.

The Coming Eclipse

The journey through the Eclipsed Lands grew ever more perilous with each step. The land was steeped in an oppressive silence, broken only by the distant sounds of the Harbinger's followers, who seemed to be closing in on them from all sides. Every shadow felt like a potential threat, every passing breeze carried whispers of dark power. Aldrin and his companions pushed forward relentlessly, the tension between them mounting as the days wore on.

They had one goal in mind to reach the ancient temple at the heart of the Eclipsed Lands, where, according to the prophecy, the hybrid king would be revealed. But with every mile they covered, the group became more fragmented, haunted by the knowledge that Ravenor's cult was everywhere.

The attacks began small—isolated skirmishes with cultists in the night, minor traps laid in their path. But soon, it became clear that these were not mere coincidences. The Harbinger's followers were watching them, stalking them, and their assaults were growing bolder, more calculated. Aldrin began to suspect that someone within their own group was betraying them, feeding information to the enemy.

As they traveled through a narrow pass, Aldrin could no longer ignore the signs. Joren, the leader of Kael's crew, had been acting increasingly distant and erratic. He had been silent for days, his once sharp gaze clouded with confusion and fear. Aldrin had seen enough to know that something was wrong.

One evening, as the group set camp under a bloodred sky, Aldrin could no longer hold back his suspicions. He pulled Joren aside, away from the others.

"You've been acting strange, Joren. We need to talk."

Joren's eyes darted nervously. "What do you mean?" he stammered, clearly uneasy.

Aldrin's voice grew cold. "I think you've been working with them—haven't you? You're under the Harbinger's influence, aren't you?"

For a moment, Joren didn't speak. Then, with a deep sigh, he dropped his gaze. "It's not that simple, Aldrin. I didn't want this. I swear."

Aldrin stepped closer, pressing him. "Then explain. Why have you been so distant? Why did you betray us?"

Joren's voice broke as he confessed. "I never meant to, Aldrin. But the Harbinger... he's not just a man. He controls minds—pulls you in with promises of power. I've been fighting it. But it's getting harder. I didn't want to betray you, but I'm caught in something much bigger than I realized."

Aldrin was silent for a long moment. He had expected a betrayal, but hearing the truth from Joren's lips struck him harder than he anticipated. Joren wasn't the villain he had assumed—he was a victim, just like everyone else caught in the web of the Harbinger's dark influence.

"I'm sorry, Aldrin. I never wanted this. But I... I can't control it anymore." Joren's voice was full of regret.

Aldrin's resolve hardened. He knew there was no time for anger or blame. Their mission had to come first. "We'll deal with this later, Joren. Right now, we need to focus on getting to the temple before it's too late."

With a final, hard look, Aldrin turned and rejoined the group. There was no time for sentimentality. They had to press forward—whatever the cost.

The group finally arrived at the ancient temple, a massive, crumbling structure that loomed against the darkening sky. The sense of foreboding that had followed them for days now seemed to suffocate them. Inside the temple, they found signs of longforgotten rituals—carvings on the walls depicting strange hybrid creatures, and offerings to an ancient god whose name had been lost to time.

But as they ventured deeper into the temple, the ground beneath their feet began to tremble. A low, rumbling sound filled the air as if the very earth was awakening. Before they could react, the doors slammed shut behind them, and an army of cultists appeared from the shadows, surrounding them on all sides.

Aldrin and Isla fought back fiercely, but the cultists were numerous, and their leader—a tall, hooded figure—stood in the center of the chaos, watching with chilling detachment. The temple seemed to collapse around them as the ground shook violently. Cracks appeared in the stone walls, and dust fell in torrents.

As the battle raged, Aldrin caught sight of a hidden doorway in the far corner of the temple, partially obscured by debris. It seemed like their only chance. He grabbed Isla's hand and pulled her toward the opening, shouting for the others to follow.

"This way!" he cried.

They barely managed to escape the collapsing temple, slipping through the narrow entrance just as the ceiling caved in behind them. The ground shook one final time, and the temple was swallowed by the earth. They were alive, but the cost had been steep.

Beneath the rubble, Aldrin and his companions found a hidden chamber—a secret altar to the hybrid king. The chamber was filled with ancient relics, all adorned with strange symbols that matched the ones they had seen on their journey. There, in the center of the altar, lay a crystal—dark, pulsing with a malevolent energy.

It was clear now. The Harbinger's plans were already in motion. The hybrid king was not just a figure in a prophecy; it was a real power that was about to be unleashed. The eclipse was almost upon them, and they had little time to stop what was coming.

Aldrin stood before the altar, his mind racing. The world was about to change. The hybrid king was no longer a distant threat—it was coming, and they had to find a way to stop it before the eclipse sealed their fate.

With a heavy heart and determination in his eyes, Aldrin turned to his companions. "We move forward. The time to stop the hybrid king is now."

The Harbinger's Reveal

The air grew thick with tension as Aldrin and his companions stood at the edge of the ancient altar, their hearts racing with the realization that they were on the verge of a momentous and terrifying event. The ground beneath their feet trembled as dark energy swirled around them, seeping from the temple's walls like a poison. The Harbinger had finally made his move.

Suddenly, the shadows that had been clinging to the edges of the temple's vast chamber surged forward, revealing themselves as the cultists—cloaked figures who had been quietly encircling them. They moved with a terrifying precision, their eyes glowing with fanatic devotion. At their head, the Harbinger emerged, his features concealed beneath a hood, his presence commanding and unsettling.

"It is over, Aldrin," the Harbinger's voice rang out, low and ominous. "The time of reckoning has come."

Before Aldrin could react, the ground before them split open with a deafening crack. From the rift, a vision manifested—a twisted, horrifying display of the hybrid king's rise to power. The vision showed a oncemortal king, now transformed by dark magic into a monstrous hybrid of man and beast, his power growing exponentially as he absorbed the life force of entire kingdoms.

In the vision, the hybrid king stood tall, his glowing eyes burning with ambition, while kingdoms crumbled before his unstoppable might. He was both man and creature—an abomination born of prophecy and bloodshed. His throne, forged from the bones of the fallen, was a symbol of his reign over a shattered world.

Aldrin felt his heart race as the truth of the prophecy settled in. The hybrid king was not some distant legend. He was real, and he was coming, fueled by the eclipse that had drawn near.

The Harbinger stepped forward, his cloak swirling like a shadow. "The hybrid king is not just a prophecy," he said, his voice like silk. "I am the one who will bring him into the world. And with him, Ravenor's true power will rise. Together, we will reshape this world."

Aldrin's mind whirled, a thousand thoughts racing through his head. This was it—the moment he had feared. The cult's plan was finally coming to fruition, and the eclipse was the catalyst. There was no time left. They had to stop the ritual—now.

But before Aldrin could act, the cultists surged forward, overwhelming them with their sheer numbers. Isla, Joren, and the others fought bravely, but it was clear that they were outmatched. Each strike from the cultists was precise and deadly, their movements guided by some unseen force. Aldrin felt the weight of his own helplessness as the cult's ritual drew closer to completion.

With a sense of desperation, Aldrin glanced at the altar where the crystal pulsed with dark energy. The sacrifice was about to be made—the hybrid king's awakening was imminent. It was then that Aldrin realized there was no more time for strategy, no more time for waiting. He had to act, or all would be lost.

In that moment of clarity, Aldrin made a choice. With a cry of defiance, he rushed forward toward the altar, his hand outstretched, his blood already beginning to boil with the energy of his decision. The cultists saw him coming and attempted to stop him, but Aldrin was unstoppable. He reached the altar and, without hesitation, slashed his own hand, allowing his blood to spill onto the stone.

The ritual faltered.

The ground shook violently, and the crystal at the altar flared with a burst of light. The cultists screamed in fury as the dark energy around them sputtered and then collapsed, unable to fully complete the awakening of the hybrid king. The power of the eclipse was disrupted, but it was not enough. The hybrid king had not fully risen, but his influence could still be felt—stronger than ever.

Aldrin fell to his knees, the blood from his wound pooling on the floor. His vision blurred as the weight of his sacrifice took hold. The ritual had been delayed, but at what cost? He could feel the blood loss draining his strength, his body fighting to remain conscious.

The cultists, now furious and disoriented, began to retreat, the Harbinger among them. His face remained hidden, but Aldrin could hear the menace in his voice as he turned away. "This is only the beginning. The hybrid king is coming, and there is nothing you can do to stop it."

As the last of the cultists disappeared into the shadows, Aldrin's companions rushed to his side. Isla, her face pale with fear, knelt beside him. "Aldrin... what have you done?"

With great effort, Aldrin forced a pained smile. "I've bought us time. But the true battle is still ahead. The hybrid king will rise again, and Ravenor's shadow will fall over us all. We must be ready."

As the echoes of the Harbinger's words faded into the distance, Aldrin felt the weight of the world pressing down on him. They had survived this battle, but the war was far from over. The kingdoms of the world were on the brink of destruction, and the true power of the hybrid king was still waiting to be unleashed.

In the quiet aftermath of the battle, Aldrin reflected on the sacrifices made—Kael's death, the loss of countless lives, and the price he had paid for this brief respite. He realized that the path ahead would not be easy. The true test had only just begun, and the kingdoms were not prepared for the coming storm.

With a final glance at the shattered altar, Aldrin spoke softly. "We move forward. Together."

The eclipse was still coming.

The Gathering Storm

The sky above the Eclipsed Lands began to clear, the eclipse slowly fading into the past, but its effects rippled far beyond the horizon. The sun shone brightly once again, but there was a palpable shift in the world. A shadow had fallen over the kingdoms, one that would not lift so easily. Ravenor's influence had only grown stronger, and with the ritual interrupted but not stopped, the hybrid king's return seemed inevitable.

Aldrin lay in the aftermath of the battle, recovering from his sacrifice, but the physical pain was nothing compared to the weight of the choices he had made. Though he had delayed the ritual, the damage had already been done. The Harbinger had gained more followers, more power, and the world was edging closer to the darkness foretold in ancient prophecies.

As Aldrin stood, feeling the weight of his duty heavier than ever, he turned to Isla, her face grim but determined. Together, they had faced the Harbinger's wrath, but now the true test awaited them.

"We must unite the kingdoms," Aldrin said, his voice low but resolute. "We cannot face this alone."

Isla nodded, her gaze unwavering. "The war is coming, Aldrin. We need every ally we can find, every strength we can muster."

The sun had set, and the night stretched out before them like an endless ocean. The Eclipsed Lands, once a place of mysterious power and danger, now seemed like a dark reflection of the world at large. Ravenor's influence had spread like a disease, and the hybrid king, though not yet fully awakened, was already a looming presence.

The sacrifice made, the battle fought, but the war—this war—had only just begun.

As Aldrin and Isla made their way back to their ship, the remnants of Kael's crew rallied behind them, their faces grim but hopeful. Joren had shown loyalty, his past shadowed by manipulation, but now he stood with them, determined to make things right.

"Onward," Aldrin murmured, his heart heavy but his spirit resolute. "We fight together."

The world trembled with the impending storm. In the distance, the first whispers of the hybrid king's rise could be heard. The final battle for the fate of the kingdoms was approaching, and the gathering storm would soon sweep across the lands, tearing apart everything they knew.

But as the ship set sail, Aldrin's thoughts lingered not just on the looming conflict, but on what lay ahead—what the world would look like once the storm had passed. Would they succeed in uniting the kingdoms? Would they be able to stop the hybrid king's awakening before it was too late? Or would they find themselves bowing to darkness, like so many before them?

The future was uncertain, shrouded in mystery and shadow, and yet Aldrin couldn't shake the feeling that something more was at play. As much as he feared the unknown, there was an undeniable curiosity that stirred within him—what would the world become after this war? Would there be light at the end of it, or would they be consumed by the darkness Ravenor sought to unleash?

The path ahead was fraught with danger, but with each new challenge, they drew closer to the truth. The storm was only beginning, but Aldrin couldn't help but wonder could they alter the course of fate, or was the future already set?

The shadow of Ravenor loomed large, but the light of their defiance burned brighter, even if the journey ahead was uncertain. And so, with heavy hearts and uncertain futures, they sailed onward—toward the unknown, and the storm that would change everything.

The Shattered Crown

Echoes of War

The war that once seemed distant now looms closer than ever. The kingdoms, though battered and fractured, are beginning to stir as the shadows of Ravenor and the hybrid king grow ever more menacing. Tensions mount between the realms, alliances crumble, and whispers of betrayal fill the air. Yet, amidst this chaos, an ancient force begins to awaken—one that could alter the very balance of the world.

Aldrin and Isla, though weary from their past battles, know that the world is standing on the precipice of total collapse. With the hybrid king's power still growing, the time to unite the kingdoms has arrived, but the road to unity is paved with treachery, deceit, and longforgotten legacies.

And within the heart of the Eclipsed Lands, a relic thought lost to time stirs once more. The Shattered Crown—the symbol of a oncegreat kingdom—beckons, and with it, the promise of a king who could either lead them to salvation or doom them all.

As the darkness spreads, the kingdoms must decide will they rise to face their greatest challenge, or will they fall, one by one, beneath the shadow of Ravenor's might?

The Call to Unity

Months have passed since the harrowing events in the Eclipsed Lands, and the oncethriving kingdoms of the known world now teeter on the edge of war. Solara, a beacon of strength in the storm, stands firm, but beneath its towering spires and marble walls, a deep divide festers. King Alaric, the stalwart ruler of the kingdom, has seen his reign tested by the loss of vital alliances, the weight of countless sacrifices, and the encroaching darkness of Ravenor's influence. The kingdom remains united in name only, as its people, once proud and unwavering, now whisper of betrayal and fractured loyalties.

The Kingdom of Tides, ravaged by the aftermath of the Leviathan's terrifying rise, lies in ruin. Queen Seris, a ruler whose strength once matched the relentless waves of her kingdom's shores, now struggles to keep her fractured lands from falling into anarchy. The people of Tides are divided—some have pledged their loyalty to her, others to the chaotic forces that seek to overthrow her rule. With the Leviathan's devastation still fresh in their memories, many fear the rise of the hybrid king and the return of Ravenor's shadow.

Aldrin returns to Solara's capital after his harrowing journey through the Eclipsed Lands, his heart heavy with the weight of countless sacrifices. His body bears the scars of battle, but it is his mind that carries the heaviest burden. The vision of the hybrid king's rise, the growing influence of Ravenor's cult, and the dark prophecy that hangs over the world—these thoughts consume him. The threat of the hybrid king's awakening grows ever more real, and his uncertainty about the future deepens. He longs for clarity, but the future is shrouded in darkness, as though the world itself has forgotten how to hope.

With each passing day, the kingdoms grow more unstable. The kingdoms of the Sea, of the Desert and the Underworld, once bound by common interest and shared alliances, now stand on the precipice of allout war. The oncepowerful leaders, bound by centuries of tradition, now find themselves scrambling to protect their fragile thrones. Every movement, every decision is watched with suspicion. The ancient bonds between the rulers have been severed, and new alliances form in secret—alliances built on the thirst for power rather than the necessity of survival.

King Alaric, wise and battlehardened though he may be, knows that something must be done to unite the kingdoms before Ravenor's influence can grow beyond control. He calls a council—an assembly of the realm's most powerful and influential leaders. The future of the known world rests on the success of this gathering, for the darkness is moving like a shadow across the lands, whispering promises of destruction and ruin. The time for alliances forged in the heat of battle, for old grudges to be forgotten, has come.

Aldrin, ever loyal but burdened by his own doubts, is summoned to attend this council. He is not merely a messenger this time; he is a voice of reason, a representative of Solara's power and his father's will. His task is clear unite the fractured kingdoms in the face of the growing storm. Yet as he rides through the capital toward the council hall, a sense of foreboding clings to him. He knows this will not be easy. The leaders of the other kingdoms—each with their own histories, ambitions, and secrets—are not quick to embrace unity. Each of them carries the weight of their own people's fears, and Aldrin's name is far from beloved in some circles.

As Aldrin walks into the grand council hall, the murmurs of the gathered rulers fall into an uneasy silence. The high walls of the chamber echo with the sounds of distant thunder as the sun begins to set behind the massive windows. There, in the center of the room, stands his father—King Alaric—his once youthful face now etched with the lines of care and weariness. His expression is unreadable, and the weight of the world seems to rest upon his shoulders.

The council begins with words of caution. Some rulers speak of their people's distrust of the other kingdoms; others question whether uniting in the face of Ravenor's rising darkness will even make a difference. Old enemies voice their displeasure with Solara's growing influence, and whispers of betrayal lurk in every corner of the room. It becomes clear that the road to unity will be far harder than Aldrin had hoped. His own position is fragile; some see him as the son of a great king, while others view him with suspicion. Even within Solara's walls, there are those who would see him removed from power for their own gain.

But Aldrin knows that time is slipping away. The hybrid king's power grows by the day, and the Harbinger's influence spreads like a creeping vine through the courts of the realm. Whispers of the Harbinger's promises—of a new world order, a world where the kingdoms will kneel to the hybrid king—echo through every conversation. It is a dark power, one that promises to change the world forever.

Despite the rising tensions and growing distrust, Aldrin knows that the only way to stop Ravenor is through unity. He must convince the rulers to put aside their differences, to see the bigger picture, and to stand together against the shadow that threatens to consume them all. But the more he speaks, the more he realizes that the real battle is not just against Ravenor's cult, but against the very forces of betrayal and fear that have taken root in the hearts of the rulers.

As Aldrin looks out across the gathered council, his heart pounds in his chest. He can see it—the vision of the world standing on the edge of ruin, where even the smallest misstep could send it tumbling into darkness. The kingdoms are at war with one another already—an internal war that has been brewing for centuries. To unite them would be a miracle; to keep them united might be impossible.

Isla stands by his side, her eyes filled with quiet determination. She has always been the steady hand to his more impulsive nature, the voice of reason when all seems lost. Together, they stand as Solara's last hope, but they are not alone. Other forces, ancient and powerful, stir beneath the surface. The Shattered Crown, the symbol of an ancient, forgotten kingdom, has begun to surface once again, its call reaching out to those who still remember its power. The hybrid king's return is imminent, and as the sun sets on the world's future, Aldrin knows that the fate of all will be decided not by kings or armies, but by the choices they make in the face of overwhelming darkness.

The path to unity is uncertain, but it is the only path they have left. Time is running out, and Aldrin knows that this moment—this council, this decision—could either save them or doom them all.

The Fractured Crown

The air in the capital of Solara was thick with tension. In the grand halls, the flicker of candlelight barely illuminated the faces of the kingdom's most powerful rulers, each one shifting in their seats as Aldrin spoke of a unity that seemed more and more impossible. The walls echoed with old promises of strength and alliances, but Aldrin could feel them crumbling beneath the weight of his words. It was a battle of hearts as much as it was of steel.

But while Aldrin worked tirelessly to piece together the fractured alliances between kingdoms, Isla was drawn to something far older—something that could change the course of the conflict in ways neither of them could have anticipated.

As the sun set behind the horizon, Isla sat in the quiet solitude of the royal library, the scent of ancient parchment thick in the air. She had become obsessed with the records of forgotten kings and queens, and hidden among the brittle scrolls and dustcovered tomes, she found what she had been searching for. The Shattered Crown—the relic spoken of only in the most cryptic of texts.

The legends varied. Some spoke of a crown forged by gods, a symbol of absolute rule, while others told of its destructive power, how it had been broken to prevent the world from succumbing to its corrupting influence. Isla, however, found something even more intriguing a map. A map that led to the last known location of the crown, buried deep within the Desert of Mirages, a place as deadly as it was mysterious.

The Desert of Mirages had long been considered impassable. The scorching heat, coupled with violent sandstorms that seemed to swallow entire caravans, made it a place no sensible ruler dared to venture. It was a desert where even the bravest had vanished, their fates lost to time. But Isla knew the truth if the Shattered Crown lay hidden there, it was their only hope of uniting the kingdoms.

Yet, Isla's heart was heavy as she considered the dangers. The Shattered Crown wasn't just a symbol of power—it was a key. Its potential could change the course of history, but the risk was staggering. Ravenor's cult had grown more powerful with each passing day, and word of the crown had surely reached their ears. She wasn't the only one who sought it. Her eyes traced the intricate symbols etched into the map, a cold realization settling in. She could already hear the faint whispers of those who were after it—rogue nobles loyal to Ravenor's cause, traitors who had abandoned their oaths and had now joined the shadow that spread across the land.

The crown had to be kept out of their hands, or all hope would be lost. The stakes were higher than ever, and Isla knew that the very future of the kingdoms rested on finding it before Ravenor's followers could.

The next morning, Aldrin rode through the gates of Solara, his mind clouded with the complexities of the council and the uncertainty of the coming war. He was a king's son, a leader by blood, but the weight of leadership had never felt heavier than now. He had done all he could to unite the fractured kingdom, but something deeper was at work—something ancient and far beyond the grasp of mortal kings.

THE CHRONICLES OF THE SHATTERED CROWN 61

Upon hearing Isla's discovery, Aldrin's first instinct was to act. His father's kingdom had grown weak, its people divided, but the opportunity that Isla had uncovered could change everything. The Shattered Crown was not just a relic; it was the key to the unity they desperately needed. But the journey would not be easy. The Desert of Mirages was not a place to be taken lightly, and no one had ever returned from its heart. The risks were immense.

Despite the dangers, Aldrin understood the importance of the crown's power. If they found it, they could use it to rally the kingdoms, to forge an alliance that would stand firm against Ravenor's growing darkness. But time was slipping away. Every moment they delayed brought them closer to Ravenor's ultimate goal the awakening of the hybrid king.

Aldrin and Isla met in the royal chambers that evening, the weight of the task ahead hanging heavy in the air between them. "We cannot wait any longer," Aldrin said, his voice low and determined. "If Ravenor learns of the crown first—"

Isla cut him off, her gaze intense. "He already knows. The cult has spies everywhere."

"Then we must beat them to it," Aldrin said, his decision made. "We leave for the Desert of Mirages at once. Gather what men we can trust."

Isla nodded, a look of resolute determination in her eyes. "There's something else," she said quietly. "Ravenor's cult isn't the only force we have to worry about. The nobles who have allied with him—they're powerful in their own right. Some of them once ruled the lands where the crown was hidden. They know the desert better than anyone. If we're to find the crown before them, we'll need more than just strength. We'll need knowledge, a guide through the desert's shifting sands."

"I'll trust you to find that guide," Aldrin replied. His thoughts turned to the future, to the perilous road that lay ahead. "Once we have the crown, we'll use it to unite the kingdoms. If we can rally the rulers of Tides, the Desert, and the Underworld to our cause, we stand a chance. But if we fail..." He trailed off, unable to finish the thought.

"We won't fail," Isla said, her voice unwavering. "The crown is the key. We just have to reach it before it's too late."

As the two of them set their plans in motion, the magnitude of their task weighed heavily on them. The Desert of Mirages awaited, and with it, the possibility of salvation—or destruction. Every step taken would bring them closer to an unknown future, a future where the fate of the kingdoms hung in the balance.

The shadows of Ravenor's influence stretched across the land, and time was running out. With the Shattered Crown, they could either forge a new dawn or watch the world fall to darkness. The question now was who would claim it first?

The First Betrayal

The wind howled across the barren landscape as Aldrin and Isla, along with a small, trusted group of soldiers, rode toward the looming expanse of the Desert of Mirages. They had crossed the borders of Solara into hostile lands, each step taking them further from the world they knew, into a place where survival was more about cunning than strength. The land seemed to shift with every gust of wind, as though the desert itself was conspiring to obscure their path.

Isla, ever the scholar, had mapped their route with painstaking care, but even the most precise maps could not account for the desert's treacherous nature. As they traveled deeper into the sands, the air grew thick, the temperature soaring by the hour, and the sense of isolation became suffocating. Yet, despite the overwhelming odds against them, there was a sense of purpose that drove them forward—a singular mission that could shape the future of the kingdoms.

At the head of their small convoy, Aldrin's thoughts often wandered to the delicate balance of power between the kingdoms. The Shattered Crown held the potential to unite them, but with each passing moment, the more he realized that unity might be an illusion.

Old grudges ran deep, and the nobility, with their selfserving ambitions, were a powder keg waiting to ignite. The kingdoms were fragmented, and every move they made seemed to stir the flames of rivalry.

One figure in particular weighed heavily on his mind Lady Seraphine. She had appeared out of nowhere, offering her assistance in their search for the crown. A noblewoman from the Kingdom of Cindrel, known for its wealth and political cunning, Seraphine was not one to be underestimated. Her charm was undeniable, and her sharp intellect had proven invaluable in their planning. But Aldrin couldn't shake the feeling that there was something more beneath her polished exterior—something he couldn't quite place.

Despite the mounting pressure, Aldrin had reluctantly allowed her to join them. Her presence provided them with critical insights into the politics of the other kingdoms, and her knowledge of the desert, albeit limited, was proving useful. But deep down, Aldrin felt an unease that refused to subside.

Isla, ever perceptive, had noticed Aldrin's wariness. "You don't trust her, do you?" she asked one evening as the two of them sat near their campfire, the crackling flames casting long shadows on the desert sand.

Aldrin leaned back, gazing into the fire. "I can't quite figure her out," he confessed. "She's too polished, too perfect. It's as if she's hiding something—something I'm not seeing."

Isla looked thoughtful. "She's certainly... calculated. But in this world, can we afford to question every potential ally?"

Aldrin said nothing, his thoughts clouded. The desert stretched out before them, vast and unforgiving. They would need every ounce of strength and trust to survive what lay ahead, but he couldn't shake the suspicion that betrayal was closer than they realized.

The tension between them all came to a head when, on the fourth night of their journey into the desert, their camp was attacked. The sound of hooves pounding across the sand shattered the silence of the night. Before they could react, dark figures emerged from the shadows—cultists, their faces masked and their eyes filled with a fanatic intensity.

The attack was brutal and swift. Aldrin's soldiers fought valiantly, but they were outnumbered, and the cultists seemed to know their every move. Through the chaos, Aldrin saw a familiar figure leading the charge—Joren. Once a trusted ally, a stalwart member of Kael's crew, Joren now stood before him, his eyes cold, his demeanor twisted by the dark influence of Ravenor's cult.

"Joren…" Aldrin whispered, disbelief coursing through him. "You… you've fallen so far."

Joren's lips curled into a sadistic smile, his voice low and mocking. "You were always too naive, Aldrin. Ravenor's power has opened my eyes to the truth. You, Isla, and your kingdom are weak. This world needs a new order, and I am the one who will bring it."

Aldrin's heart sank as he realized that Joren, the man he had once fought alongside, was no longer the person he had known. This was no longer a betrayal of trust—it was the stark reminder that the darkness they faced had already corrupted one of their own.

The cultists surged forward, and in the midst of the battle, Aldrin was separated from Isla and the others. He fought with all his strength, cutting through the cultists' ranks, but the numbers were overwhelming. As he struggled to regroup, he saw Lady Seraphine, her blade drawn, fending off attackers. But in that fleeting moment, something caught Aldrin's eye—Seraphine's hand, moving swiftly to grasp something at her side. A flash of metal—a dagger.

He barely had time to react before one of his soldiers, caught by the blade, fell to the ground with a cry. Seraphine's eyes met Aldrin's for just an instant, a brief flicker of something he couldn't name. But then, she disappeared into the fray, as if she had never been there at all.

The betrayal was sharp and sudden, and Aldrin's world began to crumble around him.

In the chaos, Isla was swept away by the tide of enemies, and Aldrin, desperate, fought his way toward her. But it was too late. The cultists had already taken her, and in the moment of the greatest loss he had ever felt, Aldrin was left with a single, haunting question Who could he trust now?

The battle raged on, but it was clear that Ravenor's power was growing stronger. They had lost the battle, but the war was far from over. Aldrin's heart pounded in his chest, knowing that the desert had already claimed the one thing he couldn't afford to lose—the woman who had been his guide and his strength.

As the first rays of dawn broke over the horizon, Aldrin knew that the true fight was only just beginning. And the hardest part? The one he feared most—he no longer knew who was friend or foe

The Desert of Mirages

The sun blazed mercilessly above the Desert of Mirages, casting endless dunes of gold and brown beneath a harsh, cloudless sky. Isla's lips were cracked from thirst, her steps slow but determined as she trudged through the evershifting sands. The world around her seemed to bend and shimmer, an illusionary haze that distorted reality itself. Each gust of wind sent the sand into swirling patterns, disorienting her, making it difficult to track her path. Yet, with each step, Isla's resolve grew stronger. She could not afford to lose the trail, nor could she afford to lose hope.

Aldrin was somewhere out there—if he was still alive. She could only pray he was surviving the chaos they'd been thrown into. But the more she thought of their separation, the more dangerous the thought became. The bond they had forged through their shared trials was strong, but the desert was as treacherous as it was vast, and the cultists were not far behind.

She had little to guide her now but the ancient texts she'd discovered and the cryptic whispers of the old nomads she had encountered. Their stories spoke of the Shattered Crown, an artifact of unimaginable power, said to control the forces of nature itself. A relic forged in the heart of the desert, its creator said to have wielded the very wind and sand to reshape the land in his image. But the crown had been lost for centuries, broken into pieces and scattered across the wastelands. Each piece was more than just a key to the past—it was a key to the future, the future that Ravenor's cult was desperate to seize.

Isla's fingers brushed the edge of the map she had kept hidden in her cloak. It was stained and torn, but it had been enough to guide her here. She could feel that she was getting closer to her goal, the underground city where the first piece of the Shattered Crown was said to be hidden. Her heart raced as she followed the map's directions, knowing she had no time to waste.

As the sun began to dip below the horizon, casting long shadows across the desert, Isla finally arrived at the entrance to the underground city—an eerie, forgotten place buried beneath the dunes. The city's ruins were vast, sprawling out in all directions like a labyrinth of crumbling stone and sandchoked streets. It was as if the city had once thrived, but now only its bones remained, ghostly structures that whispered of an ancient civilization.

The entrance to the chamber that held the first piece of the Shattered Crown was hidden beneath an overgrown archway, its inscription halferoded by time. Isla moved cautiously, knowing that the deeper she ventured into this forgotten city, the more perilous the journey would become. But there was no turning back. She had to find the artifact before the cultists did.

Her hand trembled as she pushed aside a thick curtain of sand that had settled over the entrance. The air inside was stale and musty, heavy with the scent of ancient stone and decay. Torches lined the walls, flickering to life as though the very breath of the desert was calling them to illuminate the way. She pressed forward, navigating through the narrow passages, until at last, she found herself before an enormous stone door adorned with intricate carvings—symbols she had seen only in the texts she had studied.

This was it. The heart of the lost city. The final resting place of one of the Shattered Crown's pieces.

Isla's fingers brushed over the carvings, her mind racing as she tried to decode their meaning. The symbols glowed faintly under her touch, and with a sudden shift, the heavy stone door groaned and slid open, revealing a vast chamber beyond.

Inside, bathed in the flickering light of the torches, was the first piece of the Shattered Crown—a dark, jagged shard of blackened crystal. Its edges glowed faintly with an otherworldly energy, and as Isla stepped closer, she felt the pull of the power it radiated. The ground beneath her feet trembled slightly, as if the very earth recognized the significance of this ancient relic.

But as her fingers reached out to claim it, she heard the sound of footsteps approaching. Her heart lurched in her chest.

The cultists had found her.

Isla's mind raced. She couldn't fight them all—there were too many. She needed to leave before they trapped her here, before they claimed the artifact for themselves.

But it was too late. Figures in dark robes emerged from the shadows, their eyes glowing with a malevolent light. The leader, a tall figure with a mask of silver and bloodred eyes, stepped forward. "You think you can hide from us, Isla? You think the crown is yours to claim?"

Isla's breath quickened, her hand tightening around the shard. "You're too late," she said, her voice defiant even as her heart pounded with fear. "The crown's power is not yours to wield."

The cult leader's smile was cold, calculating. "The crown belongs to Ravenor. It always has."

In an instant, the cultists lunged forward, their weapons drawn, ready to strike. Isla's instincts kicked in, and she quickly unsheathed her sword, parrying the first strike with a swift motion. But the number of enemies was overwhelming, and for every cultist she felled, two more seemed to appear in the shadows.

Just as Isla was pushed back, ready to be overwhelmed, the ground beneath her feet trembled again. There was a rumble from deeper within the chamber, a sound like the groan of the earth itself awakening. Isla's eyes widened. Something was happening—the chamber was shifting, responding to the presence of the crown.

But she couldn't wait for answers. She had to survive.

With one final, desperate swing of her sword, she cut her way through the nearest cultists and sprinted toward the exit. The piece of the Shattered Crown in her hand pulsed with power, as if urging her forward. She burst into the open air, just as a terrible roar echoed from behind her.

Aldrin.

Isla's heart leapt at the sound of his voice, and she didn't look back as she sprinted toward him, the piece of the crown clutched tightly in her grasp.

They would have to face the coming storm together. But the forces of Ravenor were closing in, and the true battle for the future of the kingdoms was about to begin.

The Shattering

The journey back from the Underground City had been a tense one. Aldrin and Isla, exhausted and wary from their escape, had barely managed to evade the relentless pursuit of Ravenor's cultists. As they entered the capital, the weight of their burden—both the first piece of the Shattered Crown and the secrets they had uncovered—hung heavily on them. The city seemed darker than before, as if it too sensed the imminent chaos that was gathering on the horizon.

The sound of clattering hooves echoed through the streets as Aldrin and Isla made their way toward the castle gates. It was there that they were met by Lady Seraphine, her smile as sharp as ever. The lady had accompanied them through much of their journey, offering her counsel and aid, her presence always a source of both comfort and caution. But something about her now felt different—darker. The glint in her eyes was no longer one of solidarity but of something more dangerous, something calculated.

Aldrin felt the shift immediately. He had trusted her, perhaps too easily. The sense of unease that had been gnawing at him for weeks finally solidified into a cold truth. Lady Seraphine wasn't just a noblewoman with connections—she was a player in Ravenor's game, and she had been from the very beginning.

"Do you have it?" she asked, her voice smooth but tinged with a venomous sweetness. "The piece of the Crown? Hand it over, and we can end this war before it truly begins."

Isla's grip tightened on the piece of the Shattered Crown she had carried across the desert. The glow of the shard pulsed in her palm, an almost alive rhythm that resonated with her heartbeat. "You've been working for him all along, haven't you?" Isla's voice cracked like a whip, her eyes narrowing in disbelief.

Seraphine smiled, the mask of a gracious ally slipping away to reveal the true face of a traitor. "I have always worked for the one who promises power. Ravenor's vision is the only one worth pursuing. The kingdoms are weak, divided. They need guidance—a strong hand to lead them." She stepped closer, her gaze fixed on the shard in Isla's hand. "And I will have it. The Shattered Crown is the key to uniting everything under one rule mine."

Aldrin stepped forward, his hand on the hilt of his sword, but Isla raised a hand to stop him. She could feel the storm brewing inside Seraphine, a storm that would tear apart everything in its path. She had to be careful—had to outmaneuver her.

"You're wrong," Isla said, her voice firm. "Ravenor's vision will burn the world to the ground. The Crown isn't a tool of power—it's a weapon that can destroy everything it touches."

Lady Seraphine laughed softly, the sound echoing like the chime of a bell before a great storm. "You misunderstand. Power is not destruction—it is control. And with the Crown, I will control everything."

Before Isla could react, Seraphine's hand moved with unnatural speed, a flash of metal in the twilight. She lunged forward, striking at Isla with a dagger laced in venom. Aldrin's instincts kicked in, and he moved to intercept, his blade clashing with Seraphine's in a shower of sparks. The force of the blow sent her stumbling back, but the lady was quick to regain her footing, her eyes filled with fury and something far darker.

The fight that erupted was swift and brutal, a blur of steel and rage. Seraphine fought like a shadow, always one step ahead, her movements graceful yet lethal. Aldrin and Isla struggled to keep up with her, the Shattered Crown's piece a heavy weight between them, a symbol of both hope and doom.

Seraphine's eyes flicked to the Crown as she circled them, a twisted smile on her lips. "It's too late, Aldrin. The pieces are already falling into place. You can't stop it."

But Aldrin's gaze was fixed on her, unwavering. "I won't let you win, Seraphine."

With a final, desperate strike, Aldrin and Isla disarmed the traitor, sending her dagger skittering across the stone floor. But as she fell back, her gaze turned cold, calculating. "You may have won this battle, but the war is far from over."

As Aldrin and Isla caught their breath, the ground beneath them trembled, a deep rumble rising from the earth itself. The Shattered Crown, even in its incomplete state, was far more powerful than they had ever realized. And in the chaos of their fight, the piece in Isla's hand was torn from her grip, the fragment of the Crown flying from her palm in a burst of light.

Aldrin reached out, but the piece shattered midair, scattering into multiple fragments, each piece disappearing into the world. The crown was no longer whole, but now more dangerous than ever—its power unleashed, its pieces scattered far and wide, and no one could predict what its next phase would bring.

In the aftermath, silence filled the courtyard. Aldrin stood with Isla by his side, both realizing the weight of their failure. Seraphine, though temporarily defeated, had already set into motion a far greater scheme, and now the Crown's pieces were scattered across the land. Their quest had become even more perilous, and the road ahead was clouded with uncertainty.

The only thing they knew for sure was that Ravenor's grip on the kingdoms was tightening. The true power of the Shattered Crown could be the key to their survival—or their ultimate destruction.

"We have to find the rest of the pieces," Isla said, her voice resolute despite the doubts that filled her heart. "The world is on the brink. We can't afford to fail now."

Aldrin nodded grimly. "Then we begin again. This war isn't over."

But as they turned to leave, the shadows of the coming storm stretched long and dark behind them. Ravenor's shadow was vast and relentless, and the race to piece together the Shattered Crown had only just begun.

The Awakening

The sun hung low over the horizon, casting long shadows over the wartorn lands. The kingdoms, already fractured by years of conflict, now stood on the precipice of total annihilation. The Shattered Crown, once thought to be nothing more than a relic of a forgotten age, had become the focal point of a battle that would decide the fate of the world. Its pieces, scattered across vast and dangerous lands, had drawn everyone into a relentless pursuit—some seeking power, others seeking salvation.

Aldrin stood at the edge of the battlements, staring out at the growing storm clouds. He could feel the shift in the air—the tension, the weight of the coming conflict. The world was holding its breath, waiting for the inevitable clash between light and shadow, between those who sought unity and those who would destroy it.

Isla joined him at the wall, her presence a quiet comfort in the midst of the storm. She didn't speak immediately; neither of them needed to. The air was thick with unspoken thoughts, fears, and the realization that their journey was far from over. The final piece of the Shattered Crown had been found, and the pieces had come together, but they were still far from understanding the full extent of its power—or the price that would have to be paid to wield it.

"We've come so far," Isla said, her voice barely more than a whisper. "But I don't know if we're ready for what's coming."

Aldrin turned to her, his expression worn but resolute. "None of us are ready. But we've come this far because we have no other choice."

The war had taken everything from them—friends, allies, trust—and it had pushed them all to their limits. The shadow of Ravenor loomed larger with each passing day, his influence spreading like a dark stain across the kingdoms. His cult had grown more powerful, more organized, and they now controlled more than ever before. But the Shattered Crown, once broken and lost, now held the key to either their salvation or their damnation.

Aldrin's mind turned back to the path that had brought them here the relentless pursuit of the crown's pieces, the battles fought in the deserts, the betrayals that had torn their allies apart, and the looming specter of the hybrid king—the one who could either unite the kingdoms or plunge the world into darkness. Each decision, each sacrifice, had led them to this moment.

Isla was right. They weren't ready. But they were the last line of defense against Ravenor's growing power. And that knowledge burned brighter than any fear they might have felt.

"We need to prepare," Aldrin said finally. "Ravenor won't wait. The final battle is coming, and with it, the choice of what kind of world we'll leave behind."

The Shattered Crown, now whole once again, rested in Aldrin's hands, its cold, ancient metal a stark reminder of the weight they carried. Its magic pulsed with a strange, alien energy, as if it recognized its own significance. But Aldrin could feel the darkness within it, the power it held to reshape the world in Ravenor's image—or in his own.

They had no way of knowing what would happen when the crown's power was unleashed, but they could no longer afford to wait. The kingdoms had been fractured for too long. Ravenor had exploited those divisions, manipulating factions and sowing chaos at every turn. The future was uncertain, and the price of victory seemed too high for anyone to bear.

But Aldrin could see no other path.

"I have to do this," he said, his voice low but filled with conviction. "I have to put an end to this. Once and for all."

Isla nodded, her eyes dark with the same uncertainty he felt. "We'll stand with you. Whatever happens, we're in this together."

The storm continued to churn on the horizon, a visible manifestation of the chaos that had overtaken the world. In the distance, the armies of Ravenor were gathering, and with each passing moment, the armies of the kingdoms were following suit. The final showdown was near, and the fate of the world rested in the balance.

As night fell, Aldrin and Isla made their way to the war council. The room was filled with the leaders of the remaining kingdoms—some reluctant, others eager, but all fearful of what the coming battle would bring. The time for diplomacy was over. Ravenor's forces were on the move, and their only hope was to unite their forces in a lastditch effort to drive him back.

The room fell silent as Aldrin stepped forward, holding the Shattered Crown before him. "This crown represents the past—our history, our unity, and our failures. But it also represents our future. The power to defeat Ravenor lies in this, in what we choose to do with it."

The leaders of the kingdoms exchanged wary glances, each one wrestling with the implications of Aldrin's words. They had all suffered losses. Some had already seen their cities fall to Ravenor's forces. Others had been forced to make compromises with the cult, too afraid to fight.

But now, with the crown before them, the choice was clear they could either stand united or fall divided.

The council erupted in heated debate, but in the end, it was the realization of the truth that bound them together. Ravenor's shadow was too large to ignore. The cost of not fighting was far greater than the cost of facing him.

And so, the kingdoms rallied under a single banner. The Shattered Crown, once a symbol of division and decay, had become the unifying force they needed to confront Ravenor. But as they prepared for the battle to come, Aldrin could feel the weight of the decision settle upon him.

The storm was coming. The final battle for the fate of the world was about to begin. And whatever happened, there would be no turning back.

The awakening of the Shattered Crown had begun.

The Last Light

The world stood still, as if holding its breath, suspended in the balance between light and shadow. The kingdoms, once proud and united under banners of old, now stood fractured and divided, each struggling with their own fears, their own weaknesses. And at the center of it all, the Shattered Crown, a relic of untold power, pulsed with an eerie energy—a force that promised either salvation or destruction.

Aldrin and Isla stood side by side on the high balcony of the wartorn capital, gazing out over the battlefield below. The horizon, once vibrant with the glow of a hopeful dawn, now seemed darkened by an impending storm. The final battle loomed on the horizon, a confrontation that would decide the fate of the world. Ravenor's forces had gathered in full, and his influence was now a shadow stretching over every kingdom, every stronghold, every soul.

The Shattered Crown was nearly complete. The pieces had been brought together through blood and sacrifice, through alliances forged and broken, through the lives of many lost along the way. But even as the crown shimmered with its newfound power, there was still doubt. Was the crown a tool of salvation, or was it a weapon that would undo everything they had fought for?

Isla, her hand resting lightly on the hilt of her sword, turned to Aldrin. Her face was set with determination, but her eyes betrayed the fear that lurked just beneath the surface.

"The last light is fading," she said quietly, the weight of her words hanging heavily between them. "Do you believe we can win this?"

Aldrin stared out over the battlefield, his thoughts a tumultuous storm of doubt, hope, and regret. He had never been a man of easy answers, but the truth was clear the time for second chances was long past. The world had come to the edge, and there would be no turning back once the storm began.

"I don't know," he said, his voice steady but tinged with the weariness of the journey. "I don't know if we can stop Ravenor. I don't know if the crown is our salvation, or our doom. But I do know one thing we must try. For the kingdoms. For the people who are still out there, waiting for hope."

Isla nodded, her grip tightening on her blade. She had seen the toll this war had taken on him, on all of them. But there was no time for rest, no time for hesitation. The battle was coming, and the future was uncertain.

The sun dipped lower, casting a long shadow across the land. The last remnants of light fought to hold their ground against the encroaching dark. In the distance, the first signs of Ravenor's army were visible—dark banners fluttering in the wind, the grim march of soldiers eager for conquest.

Aldrin turned to Isla, his eyes filled with the weight of everything they had endured. "We have one last chance. If we fail now, there may be no future at all."

"And if we succeed?" Isla asked, her voice a whisper.

Aldrin looked at her, his heart heavy with the burden of what lay ahead. "Then we rebuild. We find a way to live in a world that isn't ruled by darkness. We give the people a chance to hope again."

The wind picked up, carrying with it the scent of rain—a storm was coming, and it would not be kind. But even as the clouds gathered and the winds howled, there was a glimmer of light. A small flicker of hope, faint but undeniable.

The final pieces of the Shattered Crown were now within reach. With them came the power to change the world—if they could control it. But controlling that power would come at a cost. The path forward was uncertain, and the choices they made would ripple through the future in ways they could not yet foresee.

As the first drops of rain began to fall, Aldrin and Isla turned away from the balcony, their eyes fixed on the path that lay ahead. The final confrontation with Ravenor was near, and the stakes had never been higher. The world stood at a crossroads, and the last light of hope flickered against the encroaching dark.

One question remained would they be able to stop the rise of Ravenor and the hybrid king, or would the world fall into darkness forever?

The storm was coming. And with it, the dawn of a new era.

The Rise of the Hybrid King

The Storm Unleashed

The world teeters on the edge of destruction, shrouded in a storm of chaos and uncertainty. The onceunified kingdoms, proud in their histories and rich in their legacies, now stand divided—fractured by greed, ambition, and deeprooted mistrust. The streets echo with the clash of swords, the cries of the oppressed, and the murmurs of betrayal. The grand cities that were once symbols of power and culture now seem like crumbling monuments to a forgotten age. The horizon is darkened, not just by the clouds, but by the looming shadow of Ravenor, whose influence now stretches across the known world, like a silent plague spreading its tendrils into the hearts of kings and peasants alike.

And as Ravenor's cult grows, so too does the prophecy of the Hybrid King—the one destined to bring an end to all things, or to forge an empire greater than any that has come before. This king, born from the unholy union of ancient bloodlines and twisted rituals, stands at the edge of ascension. His arrival is foretold by dark oracles and feared by every ruler who has ever held a crown. The people, the very soul of the kingdoms, are torn between fear and hope—some desperate to prevent his rise, others eager to bask in the power he promises.

The Shattered Crown, a symbol of both divine rule and destructive ambition, has finally been pieced together. It is said to hold the key to the world's salvation, or its utter annihilation. Once broken, scattered across the lands like the ashes of a fallen empire, now it is whole again. Its power, dark and allconsuming, has begun to awaken. But the question remains Will it guide the kingdoms to unity, or plunge them into eternal war?

At the heart of this tempest stand Aldrin, Isla, and their allies—scarred by battles of the past, yet resolute in their determination to face the future. They are no strangers to sacrifice, having already lost so much in their struggle against Ravenor's forces. But as the storm gathers, they find themselves trapped in its very eye. Ravenor's legions are growing stronger by the day, preparing for the rise of the Hybrid King. The cult's influence now reaches deep into every corner of the known world, infecting cities and kingdoms alike with whispers of power, of a new world order under the rule of the king born of darkness.

In the shadows of the old world, a figure stirs—the Hybrid King himself. Some say he is already walking among them, a hidden force waiting for the right moment to reveal himself. Others speak of him as a legend, a being so powerful that even the gods themselves tremble at the thought of his ascension. His presence is felt in the very air they breathe, in the way the earth trembles beneath their feet, and in the dreams of those who dare to hope for something greater than what the world has become.

The kingdoms, shattered and broken, now find themselves at a crossroads. Old alliances have crumbled, and new ones are born in desperation, but trust is a currency no longer in circulation. Leaders grow paranoid, unsure of whom to trust as the stakes continue to rise. Can the fractured kingdoms unite before it is too late? Or will they fall, one by one, beneath the weight of Ravenor's darkness, consumed by the rise of the Hybrid King?

The clock ticks toward midnight, and the final confrontation begins to take shape. The world stands on the precipice, and only those brave enough to face the storm can change its course. But even as Aldrin, Isla, and their companions prepare for the war to come, the shadow of Ravenor and the Hybrid King looms larger. The fate of the world hangs in the balance, and nothing—no one—can be certain of who will stand in the end. The storm is here, and its fury will decide the future of the kingdoms, the world, and all those who live under its shadow.

The Gathering Dark

Months have passed since the climactic battle against Ravenor's forces. The world, once brimming with the possibility of change, now lies in tatters. Aldrin, though physically alive, feels the scars of war in every fiber of his being. He is not the same man who once rallied the kingdoms with hope and strength. The weight of countless battles, betrayals, and losses has aged him beyond his years. The world around him is crumbling, its foundations shaking as the nations begin to fall apart, divided by their own ambitions and fears. Yet, despite it all, a flicker of hope remains—an ember that refuses to die, even in the darkest of times.

The Shattered Crown, though reassembled, remains an enigma. Its pieces, once scattered and lost, are now brought together, but its true purpose eludes even those who have spent their lives seeking its power. What was once a symbol of unity now seems to be both a weapon and a curse. It pulses with an ancient and terrifying power, but no one—least of all Aldrin and Isla—can yet comprehend the full extent of its influence. It is both their greatest asset and their most dangerous liability. Its power is undeniable, but its true nature is still shrouded in mystery.

In Solara, the capital of Aldrin's homeland, King Alaric, now an aging monarch, stands at the precipice of war. His kingdom, once the pride of the known world, now finds itself fractured, caught between its own internal struggles and the external threat of Ravenor's encroaching darkness. Alaric's once mighty rule is slipping through his fingers, and his kingdom, though still the strongest among the fractured realms, is now divided. The call for unity has shifted from a cry for strength to a desperate plea for survival. The old alliances have begun to fray, and even those who once stood side by side with Aldrin now question their loyalties. War looms on the horizon, and the people of Solara are torn between hope and fear.

Aldrin and Isla, their bond forged in fire, are entrusted with the monumental task of leading the remaining kingdoms in the face of Ravenor's growing darkness. The two of them have become symbols of resistance, though neither is fully prepared for the weight of what lies ahead. Their determination to fight for the future of the world is matched only by the dread that gnaws at them—the world is shifting, and they are at the center of it all, struggling to hold together what is left of the realms.

But the true threat is far more insidious than anyone could have imagined. The hybrid king, a figure whispered about in fearful legends, grows stronger with each passing day. His awakening has begun, and his power spreads like a shadow over the land. Rumors swirl like wildfire, carried by the wind to every corner of the known world. Some say the hybrid king has already walked among them, taking human form and biding his time. Others speak of him as something more—an elemental force, tied to the earth itself, whose awakening could bring the world to its knees. The more Aldrin listens to the tales, the more he is consumed by the feeling that the prophecy is not just a myth—it is an impending reality.

Nightmares plague Aldrin's sleep, filled with images of a world ravaged by the hybrid king's reign. In these dreams, cities fall, armies crumble, and the very earth itself is twisted and reshaped by the king's power. It is a vision of doom, one that grows ever more vivid and real with each passing night. Aldrin tries to shake the fear, but it lingers in his mind, gnawing at the edges of his thoughts. He realizes that the world is on the brink of something far worse than anything they have faced before.

As he prepares for the war that is certain to come, Aldrin reflects on the heavy cost of their journey. His heart aches with the memory of those who have fallen, especially his brother Kael, whose death still haunts him. So many lives have been lost, sacrificed in the name of this neverending war, and Aldrin is left to wonder what it has all been for. The true cost of war, he realizes, is not just the lives lost on the battlefield, but the very souls of those who survive. He wonders if they are fighting for something that will truly bring peace—or if the cycle of destruction will only continue.

The world is darker now than ever before, but Aldrin knows that there is no turning back. The storm has been unleashed, and there is no way to stop it. The hybrid king's rise is inevitable. The question is no longer whether they will face him, but whether they can survive what he will bring when he steps into the world.

The gathering dark is only the beginning. What happens next will decide not only the fate of the kingdoms, but of the world itself. And as Aldrin and Isla stand at the precipice, looking out over a fractured realm, they understand that the coming storm may very well be the last battle they will ever face. But no matter the cost, they will fight—for their kingdoms, for their people, and for the hope that has sustained them through every trial. The time to unite is now, for the darkness is closing in, and soon it will be too late.

The Hybrid King's Legion

The rise of the hybrid king is not the work of a single, fateful moment, but a meticulous process. Ravenor, the dark puppet master, has spent years building his power, carefully placing each piece into the puzzle of the world's future with unwavering precision. His influence has spread like a contagion, infecting the hearts of the weak, the powerhungry, and those willing to trade their souls for power. The hybrid king, it turns out, is not just a ruler, but a living symbol—a creature whose very existence strikes terror into the hearts of his enemies and inspires awe in those who serve him. His myth spreads like wildfire across the kingdoms, his name whispered in dark corners, his power growing with each passing day.

The first significant blow to the kingdoms comes in the form of a cataclysmic assault on the Kingdom of Tides, once ruled by Queen Seris. This kingdom, already torn apart by internal strife and weakening from within, is now vulnerable to the full force of Ravenor's army. What had been a fractured, disorganized rebellion now takes the shape of an unstoppable juggernaut. The Legion, now a formidable force under Ravenor's command, strikes Tides with ruthless efficiency.

At the head of this attack is Lord Kaeron, the hybrid king's most trusted general. Lord Kaeron's loyalty to the hybrid king is absolute, and his reputation as a merciless tactician has earned him the title of "The Storm's Heart." A mountain of a man, Kaeron is a beast of war—a strategist whose cruelty is matched only by his devotion to his master. His forces move with terrifying precision, obliterating the last vestiges of Tides' defense and leaving nothing but ruin in their wake. The kingdom falls quickly and without mercy, its onceproud cities reduced to ash. The fall of Tides is a grim reminder of what is to come, the first domino in a chain of destruction that threatens to consume the world.

Aldrin, Isla, and their growing alliance of kingdoms quickly realize that the true strength of Ravenor's army does not lie in its sheer numbers. It is in the unity that binds the cultists and their soldiers, a unity forged from years of manipulation, deception, and bloodshed. The cultists, once a disjointed and fragmented group, have now come together under a singular purpose, their ranks swelled by the influence of the hybrid king. They are no longer a scattered collection of zealots—they are an organized, deadly force, each member committed to the cause with religious fervor. Each kingdom, city, and outpost in the known world is a potential target. The fall of Tides was only the beginning. What Ravenor's forces seek is not just the destruction of kingdoms, but the complete annihilation of the old world, ushering in a new era ruled by the hybrid king.

Aldrin's mind races with the implications of what has just occurred. He knows that Ravenor is playing a long game, one that has stretched over years, if not centuries. This attack on Tides is not the end of the conflict—it is only the beginning of something much more insidious. The kingdom of Tides is a devastating loss, but Aldrin cannot allow the grief to cloud his judgment. His kingdom, Solara, and all the others that remain are now vulnerable to the same fate. Unity, he realizes, is their only hope. But even that fragile alliance is beginning to crack under the pressure. Longstanding rivalries, old grudges, and mistrust now threaten to pull apart the fragile coalition that stands against Ravenor's darkness.

Aldrin and Isla rally their forces as quickly as they can, but the question still lingers where is the hybrid king? Ravenor's puppet may be orchestrating this destruction from the shadows, but his true presence remains a mystery. Some say he walks the earth already, in human form, biding his time. Others speak of him as a living embodiment of the elements—an unnatural force of nature tied to the earth itself, capable of reshaping the world with a single thought. The prophecy spoke of a king who would rise in darkness, but now the time for prophecy is over. The question is no longer whether he will come, but when—and when he does, what kind of world will he find waiting for him?

The storm has already arrived, and with it, the Hybrid King's Legion marches onward. The fate of the kingdoms hangs in the balance. Ravenor has begun to play his final hand, and Aldrin, Isla, and their allies must prepare for the worst—knowing that the true battle for the future of the world has only just begun. The time for answers is now, and the consequences of failure will be felt by all.

The Broken Crown

As the war escalates, the skies grow ever darker with the shadow of Ravenor's influence, and the world teeters on the brink of collapse. The scattered forces of the remaining kingdoms, though united in purpose, are slowly being overwhelmed by the relentless march of Ravenor's legions. Amidst the chaos, Isla, ever determined to find a way to turn the tide, uncovers a revelation that changes everything.

Through ancient texts and forgotten scrolls buried deep within the archives of Solara, Isla discovers that the true power of the Shattered Crown goes far beyond its ability to unite the kingdoms. The crown is not merely a symbol—it is a vessel, an ancient artifact capable of controlling the very essence of life itself. The legends speak of the crown's ability to bind the forces of nature to the will of its wearer, granting them dominion over the elements, the creatures of the earth, and even the forces of fate itself.

Isla's research leads her to a chilling conclusion The hybrid king is not just a ruler or a conqueror, but a being created from the very forces that once governed the world. He is a manifestation of the primal powers that existed long before the kingdoms rose to power. The hybrid king, with the crown in his possession, would be more than a king—he would be a living god, a creature of both human and divine origin, capable of reshaping the world to his will.

But there is more to the story—an ancient ritual lies at the heart of the crown's power, a ritual that, when completed, will awaken the hybrid king's true form. This ceremony, however, is not without a price. The ritual demands a great sacrifice—one that is not merely physical, but spiritual. To complete the awakening, a soul must be offered, a life must be taken, and a nation must be consumed by the crown's terrible power. This is the cost of controlling the forces of nature itself—an unthinkable price, one that Isla and Aldrin cannot allow to be paid.

As they grasp the gravity of this discovery, the enormity of their task becomes painfully clear. The only way to prevent the hybrid king's full awakening—and the destruction of everything they know—lies in stopping the ritual before it can be completed. But the journey to stop it will take them deep into the heart of Ravenor's domain, a place where the very laws of nature have been warped and twisted. The land itself is corrupted, the air thick with magic, and every step forward is a step closer to the edge of madness. It is a realm where the boundaries between life and death are blurred, and where the hybrid king's power is absolute.

Aldrin and Isla, joined by their most loyal allies, must venture into this cursed realm, knowing that the journey will not only take them through the heart of enemy territory but also force them to confront the darkness within themselves. The stakes could not be higher—if they fail, the world will be reshaped in the hybrid king's image, and the lands will fall into eternal darkness.

But even more personal stakes weigh on Aldrin's mind. The Shattered Crown is not just an object of power—it is a part of his legacy, a legacy tied to the very blood that flows through his veins. The crown's dark history is intertwined with his own family's past, and as Aldrin travels deeper into the heart of Ravenor's domain, he is forced to confront not only the legacy of the crown but the dark legacy within himself. The crown's power is corrupting, and it is no longer clear whether Aldrin's pursuit of victory will cost him his humanity.

Old fears and doubts, long buried, resurface within Aldrin. His nightmares grow more vivid, filled with visions of a world consumed by the hybrid king's reign, and of his own role in shaping the kingdom's fate. Is he truly the hero they need, or has he become a pawn in a far greater game—one that he may not be able to control?

With the fate of the world hanging in the balance, Aldrin, Isla, and their allies set forth on a journey fraught with peril and uncertainty. They know that their enemies are not only the forces of Ravenor but the very forces of nature itself, twisted by the hybrid king's power. Every step forward brings them closer to a truth that could either save the world or destroy it utterly.

The broken crown may be their salvation—but only if they can survive long enough to understand its true nature.

Betrayal and Sacrifice

As Aldrin and Isla march toward the heart of Ravenor's realm, the land grows darker, more twisted with every passing moment. The very air seems to pulse with malice, and the atmosphere crackles with a strange energy that distorts their senses. The journey has been long, but this final leg is the most perilous, not only because of the overwhelming dangers they face, but because of the treachery that lurks within their own ranks.

The fragile alliances they have built begin to crack under the pressure of the impending war. Trust, once an unspoken bond among their group, is now a luxury they can no longer afford. As the group draws closer to Ravenor's domain, whispers of doubt and fear spread like a contagion, infecting the hearts of those who once fought together as a united front. The uncertainty of the future becomes all too real, and even Aldrin begins to question the choices he has made along the way. His leadership, once unquestioned, is now under threat from within.

The first devastating blow comes from an unexpected quarter. Lady Seraphine, once a trusted companion, reveals her true allegiance. The noblewoman who had once aided them in their fight against Ravenor is revealed to have been working as a double agent all along, playing a long game to further the rise of the hybrid king. Her manipulation of Aldrin and Isla, her whispered promises of salvation, were nothing but tools to bring about the exact future they have been fighting against. Her betrayal is not just a blow to Aldrin's trust but to everything he has fought for—the idea that even the noblest among them could be swayed by power, greed, and fear.

Seraphine's betrayal cuts deep, and Aldrin is left shattered, his heart filled with rage and disbelief. How could he have been so blind? How could he have trusted someone who was only ever interested in her own ambitions? But in this moment of weakness, Aldrin understands something crucial the war they are fighting is not just against Ravenor, nor the hybrid king—it is a war for the soul of humanity itself. The very forces they are up against seek to corrupt and twist everything they believe in, and no one, not even those closest to them, is beyond suspicion.

In the aftermath of Seraphine's betrayal, Aldrin and Isla are forced to confront their own fears and doubts. With time running out and the hybrid king's power growing stronger, they face an impossible decision. To stop the rise of Ravenor and the hybrid king, they must be willing to sacrifice everything their alliance, their very lives, and even the essence of their humanity. The Shattered Crown, the key to the kingdom's survival, is also the key to their own destruction. The crown's power can shape the world—but it is a power that corrupts, and the cost of using it may be more than they are willing to pay.

The sacrifice required is not just a physical one but a spiritual and moral one. Aldrin, once certain of his purpose, now stands on the precipice of a fate darker than he ever imagined. To wield the crown's power, they must give up the very things that make them human—merely to have a chance at saving the kingdoms. The burden is heavy, and the cost seems too high. But they have no other choice. The fate of the world depends on their willingness to walk this path.

As they prepare for the final confrontation with Ravenor and the hybrid king, the world around them begins to unravel. The kingdoms are falling, cities are burning, and the people are filled with dread. The hybrid king's rise is imminent. His power has already begun to spread like wildfire, leaving devastation in its wake. The oncegreat kingdoms are crumbling beneath the weight of his darkness, and only a handful of brave souls stand between the hybrid king and the world's final fall into shadow.

Aldrin and Isla's bond, tested by betrayal and sacrifice, becomes stronger than ever. Yet they know that the future is uncertain, and the outcome of the final battle is not guaranteed. Their actions will either ignite the hope of the kingdoms or extinguish it forever. With the stakes higher than ever, the only question left is Will they be able to defeat the hybrid king before it is too late? Or will they fall beneath the crushing weight of his power and witness the world's descent into an endless night?

The darkness closes in, and the final battle awaits.

The Final Stand

The air is thick with tension, the very ground beneath them trembling as if in anticipation of the storm about to break. The kingdoms stand on the brink of annihilation, and the weight of this truth presses heavily on Aldrin and Isla. Their journey, fraught with sacrifices, betrayals, and loss, has led them to this moment—the final confrontation with the hybrid king, the embodiment of darkness and destruction.

The Shattered Crown, now complete, rests heavy upon Aldrin's head, its power surging through his veins. It is both a weapon and a curse, a force of unimaginable potential that could either save the world or doom it to eternal night. With every passing moment, the crown's influence grows stronger, and Aldrin feels the pull of its power, tempting him to use it to reshape the world. But with that temptation comes a terrible price—his soul, his humanity, his very essence. The crown does not simply grant power; it demands everything in return.

As the sun sets on the battlefield, the hybrid king finally reveals himself in his true form. He is both terrifying and aweinspiring—an ancient being of darkness, halfhuman and halfgod, his form shifting between the realms of reality and nightmare. His presence distorts the very fabric of existence, and the earth beneath him trembles in fear. His eyes glow with the malevolent energy of a thousand forgotten gods, and his voice is like the rumble of thunder, promising devastation.

Ravenor, his puppet master, stands in the shadows, smiling with quiet satisfaction. He has manipulated the course of history to bring this moment to fruition. The hybrid king is his creation—his legacy—and the world will bend to his will.

But Aldrin and Isla, though battered and scarred, stand resolute. The armies of the kingdoms, united in their final stand, gather behind them, ready to face the darkness. But the battle is not just one of steel and blood. It is a battle of wills—of ideologies, of belief, of who will control the fate of the world. The hybrid king believes in absolute power—rule through fear, domination through strength. But Aldrin believes in something more unity, hope, and the enduring power of the human spirit.

The clash is cataclysmic. As the armies collide, the earth shudders with the violence of the battle. The sky itself seems to burn with the fury of the conflict. The Shattered Crown hums with energy, its power threatening to tear apart the very fabric of reality. Aldrin and Isla, leading the charge, know that this will be their final test—the moment where everything they have fought for will either be realized or lost forever.

Aldrin faces the hybrid king alone, their final confrontation a battle of wills. The hybrid king speaks of the inevitability of his rise, the futility of resistance. He tells Aldrin that his vision is flawed, that the world is weak, and only through absolute power can there be true peace. But Aldrin, with every ounce of his strength, rejects this vision. He tells the hybrid king that power, in the end, is not the answer—that the world will not be shaped by force, but by the choices of its people.

As the battle rages around them, the Shattered Crown glows brighter, its energy reaching a boiling point. Aldrin feels the power within him, urging him to use it, to finish the battle once and for all. But in that moment, he realizes the true cost of wielding such power. To destroy the hybrid king, to defeat Ravenor, would mean sacrificing everything he has left—his friends, his love, his humanity.

Isla, standing by his side, calls out to him, urging him to hold on to who he is, to the very heart of what they are fighting for. Together, they make a final, desperate choice they will not allow the crown to control them. They will destroy its power, shatter it once and for all, so that the world may have a chance to rebuild.

With a final surge of strength, they shatter the Shattered Crown, its power exploding outward in a blinding flash. The earth trembles, the skies darken, and for a brief moment, everything is still. The hybrid king, his power suddenly severed, stumbles backward, his form flickering between the human and divine. Ravenor, too, falters, his grip on the world slipping away as the forces of chaos begin to unravel.

But the victory comes at a terrible cost. Aldrin and Isla, their bond unbreakable, stand together amidst the devastation, knowing that the price of their triumph was the very essence of their world. They have sacrificed the crown, the power that could have reshaped the world, for the sake of its future. The hybrid king is no more, and Ravenor's forces are scattered, defeated.

Yet, as the dust settles and the world begins to heal, Aldrin understands that the true victory was not in defeating the hybrid king, but in choosing the path of hope over power. The kingdoms, though scarred and broken, now have a chance to rebuild, to forge a new future. The final stand was not just a battle for survival—it was a battle for the soul of the world.

The final in this epic saga is not one of triumph through domination, but of triumph through unity, sacrifice, and the unyielding will to shape the future. The storm has passed, and the dawn of a new era begins.

But the question remains what kind of world will they build from the ashes of the old?

Milton Keynes UK
Ingram Content Group UK Ltd.
UKHW031046291124
451807UK00001B/90